GARY CHURCH

TEXAS JUSTICE

BARLOW
SEEKER OF JUSTICE
1881

BOOK 2

Dedication

Dan Cummings

In the challenging, complex world of educational leadership and teaching, our students and teachers need a leader who can lead in good times and bad; solve problems, build a successful team, and promote core values that focus on the success of the students.

Dan Cummings is your man.

Thanks, Dan.

Samuel Barlow -Attorney at Law, served in the Civil War

Sadie Barlow—Barlow's wife

Phoebe- Barlow's legal clerk

Tobias-Barlow's chief investigator, married to Phoebe

Nathan-Investigator, married to Elvira, Sadie's sister

Clyde—Owner of Dependable Investigations in Austin, Texas

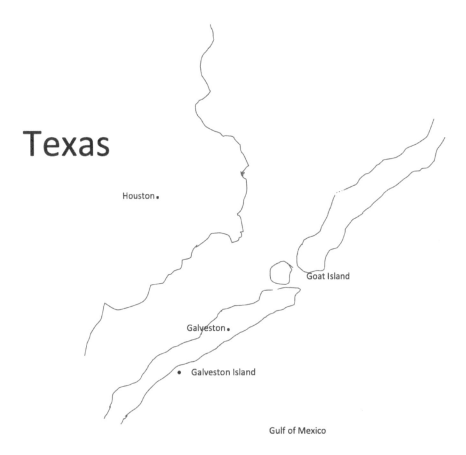

Texas

Houston.

Goat Island

Galveston.

• Galveston Island

Gulf of Mexico

PROLOGUE

Samuel Barlow, dressed for work in his customary suit and continental tie, but still in his shirtsleeves, stood quietly in the bedroom, watching his wife of two weeks, Sadie, sleep. Contrasting feelings flowed through him. He knew he was still in the first throes of happiness enjoyed by those who emotionally and romantically connected with another person, love, as it was always referred to. What had Clyde called feelings in this early state? A new word. Euphoric. He felt euphoric. He had seen it often enough, although this was a first for himself. He had come close, over five years ago, when he and Sadie had been seeing each other regularly. Perhaps because he was nearing the point where he would have to commit himself to the relationship, he had pulled away. He took up with another woman and by the time he discovered what a terrible mistake it had been, Sadie had moved on. But he was given a second chance, and he grabbed it. He had no regrets, but he was anxious. All of his life, he had enjoyed female companionship, but had never married or lived with a woman. Now, not only did he find his routine upset, he was responsible for another human being. He took his duty to his clients, and those that worked for him seriously, but this was different. Taking a wife was a lifelong and heavy obligation.

He turned and walked to the rack behind the door to get his sack coat and there, hanging beside it, was a concealed weapon shoulder holster, complete with a five shot .442 caliber British Welby Bulldog. Sporting ivory handles, the handgun and the holster rig had been a gift from Sadie.

She had given it to him, unsmiling and simply said, "Please wear it."

Last year, a man had entered his offices and would have shot Barlow had Tobias not killed the man first. Barlow guessed Phoebe had told her

1

about the incident. He had carried a gun in his boot for years and had used it occasionally, but it wasn't helpful when someone was pointing a gun at you. It was, in fact, unlawful in the state of Texas to carry a firearm, a knife or brass knuckles on one's person. It was legal to keep a weapon at home or at one's place of business. A first offense was punishable by a fine of from twenty-five to one hundred dollars. A second offense could result in a sentence of up to ninety days in the county jail. Barlow had always had a gun about his person. He figured a fine or time in the county jail was better than being dead. He strapped on the shoulder holster, pulled on his coat, stepped out, shut the door softly and took the stairs down to the lobby of the Tremont hotel, in Galveston, Texas. Galveston was a small town established as a port on an island twenty miles off the coast of Texas. Barlow had lived in the hotel since he had arrived in Galveston. Nodding to the clerk at the desk, Barlow exited and walked to the café, where he and his team met for breakfast every Monday morning.

He arrived at his usual time, but everyone was already seated. Phoebe, a beautiful former actress from New York, now his legal assistant. Tobias, a young man from Tennessee; skilled in many areas and his chief investigator, and Nathan, a young Civil War veteran, Barlow's brother-in-law and his newest investigator. Everyone appeared nervous. It was, in fact, their first meeting since Barlow hired Nathan and all of them were involved in a triple wedding. Barlow and Sadie, Nathan and Elvira, Sadie's sister and Tobias and Phoebe.

"Good morning," said Barlow, and everyone nodded and returned his greeting.

After a few minutes, things felt normal as they talked among themselves, discussing their honeymoon experiences. Barlow listened, smiled, and enjoyed his breakfast.

Phoebe asked after Sadie and Barlow smiled, and replied, "She's well."

When everyone finished and their coffee cups were refilled, Barlow said, "Everyone, the Barlow Law and Investigations Office, has been closed for fourteen days. I'm going to stop by the courthouse and let the judges' clerks and the district attorney know I'm back and we are open for business. I'll be in the office in about an hour and we'll see what comes up."

As he entered the courthouse, Barlow saw a deputy sheriff he knew, wearing his best hat, a sure sign he was there to testify in court. Barlow nodded at him, but the deputy waved him over.

With a smirk, the deputy asked, "How was the honeymoon, Barlow?"

"It was fine Dale, thank you."

"Must not been all that much fun, you back to work bright and early."

"I am; got myself a wife to support," replied Barlow, smiling. "Thought to check in with the clerks."

"Well, there's a fellow asked for you, name of Crenshaw."

Barlow's head snapped up to look Dale in the eye. "Robert Crenshaw?" Robert Crenshaw owned two ships and was a client and a friend.

Seeing Barlow's reaction, Dale quickly added, "He's not in trouble. He was at the jail visiting one of his boys. Stabbed a fellow to death in a bar fight a couple of days ago. I told Crenshaw you'd be back in a few days. He went over to see the district attorney and told him his boy weren't to be bothered until you got back."

"Appreciate it," replied Barlow, continuing on to the judge's offices to tell the court clerks he was back at work, his thoughts on the Crenshaw boy, sitting in jail, possibly facing death by hanging for killing a man in a bar fight.

CHAPTER 1

Much to his surprise, Barlow found his law office full of people when he entered. He stood still, looking around, as Phoebe rose, strove to him and escorted him to his private office, closing the door behind her.

She smiled broadly. "You are in demand, Barlow."

Barlow smiled. "I know you like to see me busy. You'll be pleased to know we're likely to be retained for a criminal case," he responded.

Phoebe, his legal assistant, secretary and receptionist, who kept up with expenses and income with a vengeance, replied, "Can the accused pay?"

"As a matter of fact, they can. It's one of Robert Crenshaw's boys. He's accused of stabbing a man to death in a bar fight. Please send someone to tell Robert I'm in the office and I will see him as soon as he can get here. Say, was that Tobias and Nathan I saw?"

Phoebe laughed. "Yes, don't they look nice in their new suits? Elvira and I decided they needed to look a bit more professional."

It was Barlow's turn to laugh. "I didn't recognize them right off."

"I'll send a message to Mr. Crenshaw's office, but meanwhile, the elderly couple were waiting outside when I got here. You should see them first. They have a letter demanding they vacate their home and ranch in thirty days. Likely they owe the bank, and they are very upset."

Phoebe introduced Barlow to the couple, Eb and Geneva Wardlow. Both were wearing their Sunday church clothes, but their dark, leathery skin made their vocation clear.

After everyone was seated, Barlow asked, "How can I help you folks?"

"Well, sir, we transferred the deed to our ranch and now we have a hell of a problem," said Eb, earning himself a stern look from his wife.

4

"Language, Eb," she muttered.

"We signed all the paperwork transferring the property, but we were supposed to stay put, you know, live on our homestead, until we are both dead. Now, we got this here notice saying we have thirty days to vacate the house and land. That was ten days ago. I mean, it's our place. How can they do that?" Barlow started to speak, but Eb raised his hand. "We done been to three other lawyers and they say there ain't nothing can be done. A lady you helped told Geneva to see you so we're here, hoping there is something can be done."

"You got to help us, Mr. Barlow," said Geneva. "We've some money saved, and we can pay your fees, but we don't want to leave our home."

"Of course, where is your ranch located?"

"In Galveston County, on the other side of the bay," replied Eb. "We're south of Clear Creek. It's about five miles to town, course it ain't much of a town."

"Are you behind on property taxes?"

"Why no, I got all the receipts," said Geneva.

"I see, well how much do you owe the bank against your place?"

Eb and Geneva looked at each other. "That's the thing," said Eb, "We don't owe any money to anybody. It's all bought and paid for. All six hundred acres."

Barlow prided himself on his control, but his face expressed surprise. "You sold your ranch; with the condition you could live there until you both passed?"

"No sir, we didn't want no money, just transferred the deed," stated Eb.

Barlow frowned. "Do you have a copy of the paperwork? Perhaps the contract giving you the right to remain on the property until your death?"

"No sir, there weren't no papers on that. That was all understood, when we talked about the transfer."

Barlow's face tightened, but he wasn't worried. No court in the land would accept that someone would knowingly give away a six-hundred-acre ranch. There was something wrong, but as with most clients, he had to draw the story out of them.

"Did a lawyer handle the sale for you?"

Once again, Eb and Geneva looked at each other.

"We didn't reckon on needing our own lawyer," said Eb. "We figured, you know, we trusted 'em. A lawyer in Houston did the paperwork."

Barlow's mouth tightened. "I see. But I still don't understand why you would give up your ranch for nothing, even if you meant to keep living there, rent free."

"Mr. Barlow, I'm sorry, we weren't clear," said Geneva. "We're anxious and not thinking straight. What happened, is our son, DeWayne. Well, we have in our will to leave everything to him when we die. But he and his wife, Lavinia, was saying how it was best if we transferred the property into DeWayne's name now, so when we die they won't have no trouble. So that's what we did, but they said we would keep living there and working our place until we died. Then we got this notice. We ain't been able to find Lavinia or DeWayne, so we went to a lawyer. He said nothing we could do, so we tried others who said the same thing."

"Your son is behind this?" asked Barlow.

"The last lawyer told us it was him filed to have us evicted from our place," said Eb, meekly.

Barlow sat perfectly still. He thought he had heard just about everything, but he had been wrong. Finally, he said, "I'll look into the situation. If I think we can help you, I will take on the case."

Eb and Geneva looked at each other and Geneva burst into tears.

Barlow stood, walked to the door, opened it and nodded at Phoebe, who rose and came to speak to him. "Can you send the Wardlows down to the Island Café and tell them Nathan and Tobias will be along to speak to them in a few minutes?"

As Phoebe escorted the still crying Geneva and Geneva's husband Eb out of Barlow's office, Barlow caught Tobias's eye and motioned with his head for him to join him.

As Tobias entered his office, Barlow closed the door, and the two stood just inside it.

"Those folks are the Wardlows. Geneva and Eb. At their son's and daughter-in-law's urging, they signed over the deed to their ranch to the son, DeWayne. Now, they haven't seen him for a while and he has filed for an order to have them removed from their home."

Tobias's face registered shock.

"I want you and Nathan to meet them at the Island Café and find out everything you can about the son and his wife. Then find them. Don't contact them, I just want to know how to locate them for now."

Tobias nodded, opened the door and with a glance and a smile at Phoebe, he waved come-on at Nathan, hesitating only for a second to grab his hat off the rack by the door.

Tobias and Nathan found the Wardlows waiting at the café, as Phoebe had asked. After introductions, Tobias explained. "Mr. Barlow wants us to find your son. If you will tell us all you can think of about him and his wife it will us find him. What he likes to do, who his friends are. That sort of thing."

"He likes to fish," said Eb. "Leastwise he done, till he got married."

"He's a reader. Has been since he was a kid," added Geneva. "He's a sweet boy."

"A hard worker, too," said Eb, with some excitement in his voice.

"He was shy with girls. Never really had a steady girl," said Geneva.

Tobias and Nathan stole a glance at each other. This sure didn't sound like a cold-blooded son who would turn his own parents out of their home.

"Till he met Lavinia," added Eb. "That's his wife."

"They met at church," said Geneva. "They are so happy. We just don't understand what's happening. Maybe some bad men are making DeWayne do this. It's the only way, really. You must find him."

"I'm sure we'll find him soon. Tell me, is he fond of drinking?" asked Tobias.

"Why no. He don't drink or gamble. I told you he's a church going God-fearing young man. If we can just talk to him, I'm sure we can settle this silliness about us having to move out of our house."

"Did you say DeWayne enjoys fishing?" asked Nathan.

"Aw, well, me and him, we used to go fishing every Saturday night, come hell or high water," said Eb.

"Eb! What has gotten into you?" exclaimed Geneva.

"Sorry, I meant, no matter what, DeWayne and I would go fishing on Saturday nights. We hardly missed a trip. But after he got to calling on Lavinia, he'd do his work on the ranch, but on Saturdays, as soon as he was finished, he'd take off. He wouldn't show up till breakfast on Monday. Stopped showing up at church. We ain't been fishing since he met her."

Nathan smiled. "Yes sir. I reckon that's understandable."

"What can you tell us about Lavinia?" asked Tobias.

Eb looked at Geneva, who frowned, then said, "We know little. She came out to the house twice for supper and we saw her and DeWayne at church a few times. Like I said, DeWayne met her at church. We attend the First Baptist in Clear Creek. She said she was a teacher in Houston, but she her daddy died in the War, and her mother died afore Christmas, so she came down to Clear Creek to stay with her brother."

"What is her brother's name?" asked Nathan.

"Smith," answered Geneva.

Tobias let out a quiet sigh. Smith was a very common name. "Do you know her brother's given name or where he lives?" he asked.

Geneva shook her head. "They just showed up one Sunday evening, saying they had got hitched. We asked about the brother, but she said he quit his job at the brick factory and went to live with a cousin in Houston. DeWayne said he was gonna get on with the brick factory and they was gonna live in Lavinia's brothers' house. We never visited her. She always came out to the house, or DeWayne went to see her. Then one Sunday night they come out to the house and talked to us about signing over the place. We met at a law office in Houston to do that."

"Can you describe Lavinia?" asked Nathan.

"She talks funny," said Eb.

"She's beautiful," said Geneva.

"She has scary eyes," said Eb.

After giving Eb another stern look, Geneva said, "Her eyes are black, and she has an accent, but she speaks English well enough. DeWayne is twenty-two, and she said she was twenty."

"Is she Mexican?" asked Tobias.

"No, I reckon she's from somewhere in Europe," answered Geneva.

"Well, I guess that's it for now. Give us directions to your ranch so we can find you if need be. If you hear from DeWayne, please send word to the office."

"We surely will," replied Eb, as Geneva called to the waitress for a pencil.

As they left the café, Tobias looked at Nathan and asked, "What say we grab the Houston train, get off at Clear Creek?"

Nathan smiled.

CHAPTER 2

Barlow saw a dozen clients before noon. Most were routine matters, wills, contracts, and civil disputes. He had declined to represent an accused horse thief, who admitted his guilt to Barlow. It surprised the man when Barlow told him he would not agree to be his lawyer, but he recommended a fellow attorney. Phoebe made appointments for several more potential clients, and the last one had just left when Barlow stepped out of his office.

"What say we eat dinner together," said Barlow. "I could use a break."

Phoebe frowned. "We might miss some business," she said.

"We'll put a note on the door," responded Barlow, smiling.

Phoebe eyed Barlow for a minute before agreeing. "Fine, but we must eat quickly."

Four people were waiting when the pair returned from their noon meal, including a boy with a note for Barlow. Barlow took the note, read it, handed the boy two bits and said, "Tell the man that sent you that three o'clock is fine."

"Yes sir," said the boy, turning quickly, and in a second, he could be heard bounding down the steps.

"Robert Crenshaw," said Barlow to Phoebe, who nodded.

Phoebe spoke to the three people waiting and ushered one man into Barlow's office. An hour later, they were still busy, with four men waiting and two in Barlow's offices, when a woman walked in the door. She stood, looking around. Phoebe noticed her and instantly assessed her. Pretty, young, expensive dress and very expensive hat.

Standing and approaching the woman, Phoebe said, "Good afternoon."

The woman waved a dismissive hand at Phoebe. "I'm looking for Tobias, but I don't see him. Is he still out of town?"

"He is unavailable, but perhaps I can be of help," said Phoebe, her voice businesslike and crisp.

Sighing, the woman looked at Phoebe. "I am worried about him. He said he was going out of town on business, but that was a month ago."

"What is your name, if I may ask?" said Phoebe, her voice turning pleasant.

"It's Mary Beth," said the woman, her face featuring a false smile. "When will Tobias return?"

"I can't say. Our work here is confidential," replied Phoebe, "but I will tell him you asked after him."

The false smile on the woman's face faded. "I must insist that you tell me where he is and when he will return. No, I want to talk to your boss, Barlow, is it?"

The four men sitting in the room, waiting, were enjoying the show.

"Mary Beth, I can make you an appointment with Mister Barlow, if you'd like. We have some openings next week."

Her face turning red, Mary Beth responded, "Tobias will be very upset when he hears how you've treated me."

"If there is nothing else, I must return to my work," said Phoebe.

"I don't think you understand," hissed the woman. "Tobias and I are practically engaged."

"I'll tell him you came by when I see him at supper. Have a good day," replied Phoebe, turning and walking back to her desk, leaving the woman standing in the middle of the room.

"What is your name!" demanded Mary Beth.

Turning to face the woman, Phoebe said calmly, "Phoebe Shelton."

Mary Beth frowned. Several seconds passed. The women stared at each other. Finally, Mary Beth spoke. "Are you Tobias's sister or something?"

"No, I'm his wife," replied Phoebe.

When Mary Beth slammed the door shut, Barlow stuck his head out of his office and looked around, then pulled his head back inside and closed his door.

After being humiliated by that awful woman at the Barlow law office, Mary Beth spent the rest of the day in her room crying, after telling her mother she wasn't feeling well. *She and Tobias had been having such a grand time. How could he have married another woman? Maybe the woman was lying. Of course, she thought, the woman was simply an evil, demented witch who wanted to drive Mary Beth away.*

After washing her face, Mary Beth told her mother she was feeling better and going for a walk. She arrived at the Barlow Law Office late that afternoon and waited across the street in the shadows. Finally, she saw the woman who called herself Phoebe Shelton come out onto the street. Mary Beth followed her home and waited outside, watching, but she saw no sign of Tobias. Either he was out of town or he wasn't married.

CHAPTER 3

Robert Crenshaw's face reflected his worry and the stress he was under. He was sitting in Barlow's office in one of the client chairs. Barlow was behind his desk, studying Crenshaw and listening.

"Thanks for seeing me Sam, I've got to get my boy out of jail and get this thing settled."

"Tell me what you know," said Barlow.

"It's Earl, my youngest. A fine young man." Crenshaw seemed to become lost in thought, then continuing, "He works in the offices with me. Good with figures. Never been in trouble."

Barlow didn't speak, but kept his focus on Crenshaw, letting him tell the story.

"He always leaves early Saturday afternoons. I encourage him to. He works hard and doesn't cause me any grief. He runs with two or three boys his own age. They like to go out to the Wild Horse Saloon. You know it?"

"I've had a few clients that frequented the place," said Barlow, smiling.

"I've not been there myself, but I understand a fair number of loose women frequent the place. Well, he's a young man. I don't judge him. Anyway, he'll have to tell you what happened. I wouldn't let him tell me, what with who knows what ears are about, but the sheriff said Earl was there Saturday night with his friends and a fight broke out. He's charged with stabbing a man to death, but he's not the violent type, Sam. I mean, he'll fight if he has to, but he isn't one to seek trouble. And stabbing a man. I don't believe it. Not for a minute."

"I'll go see him after we finish up today and see if the judge will set bail first thing in the morning," said Barlow. "The district attorney will present the case to a grand jury in a week or two, and if he's indicted, his bail might be rescinded."

"Thank you. As you know, money is not a problem. Just get him out of jail and please, Sam. I couldn't live knowing he was in that hellhole in Huntsville. I've heard the stories. They treat convicts like they aren't human. I'd almost rather they hung him. It would kill me, just quicker."

Tobias and Nathan had not returned by the end of the day. Barlow shooed Phoebe out of the office and locked up just after six that evening. On the way to the jail, Barlow thought about the terrific strain Robert Crenshaw must be under. Barlow didn't have children, but he understood the pain that parents felt when something affected their children. He had witnessed it often enough. First, in the War, then as an attorney.

Twenty minutes later, Barlow was seated at a table in the jail, Robert Crenshaw's son, Earl, seated across from him. "I'm Sam Barlow, an attorney. Your father has hired me to represent you, Earl. Any objections?"

"No sir," replied Earl. "When can I get out of here?"

"Tomorrow, if all goes well. Now how about you tell me what happened?"

"Well sir, me and two of my friends, Ned and Lou, we like to have a beer or two on Saturday night. Sometimes we go out to the Wild Horse." He became silent, seemed lost in thought.

"I understand," replied Barlow, encouraging the young man to continue.

"Saturday, we had a few beers at Al's place and played some faro. Then we went out to the Wild Horse. I'm not sure what happened. I was at the bar, Ned and Lou was upstairs, you understand?"

Barlow nodded, and asked, "Was the place crowded?"

"Yes sir, it was. Any no how, I was pretty drunk I guess and these two fellows next to me started arguing, foreigners. I couldn't understand a word they was saying. Then a fight broke out. I tried to get out of the way, but somebody grabbed me and kind of pulled me away from the bar and into the brawl." Earl hesitated, thinking, and then continued, "It was a jumble of people fighting, yelling, and cursing. I remember hitting the floor and somebody stomping on me."

Earl said nothing for a full minute. Finally, Barlow said, "Were you able to get up?"

His head snapped up to look at Barlow, as though he was just realizing he was still there. "Yeah, I got up, but there was people all around me, wresting and fighting. Cursing. I heard a gunshot. Sounded like a scattergun. Everything went quiet. Somebody kicked me; then I was pushed. I fell on top of a fellow."

"I'm following you," said Barlow, in a quiet, calm voice.

"They use kerosene lamps there. It was pretty dark in the middle of the room. The bartender had fired a gun right out an open window at the end of the bar. It worked. The fighting stopped. I got to my feet and hobbled back to the bar; I was hurting something fierce from being kicked in the ribs. It was really dark. Some lamps had gotten broken, and I saw the guy on the floor, but figured he was passed out or knocked out. My beer was still there on the bar, but when I picked it up, I saw blood on my hand and my shirt sleeve. Then I felt it on my shirt. I finished my beer pretty quick and left instead of having another. I figured no telling how long Ned and Lou would be. They got a place out back for horses, so I made my way out and found my horse."

Earl stopped talking, sighed.

Barlow studied him. His thought was that the boy was being truthful. "Go on."

"I went home. Put my horse in the corral, and went to bed. Next day was Sunday, so I didn't have to work. I was still in bed when there was pounding on the door. I got up and answered it. Two deputies was there and told me I was under arrest on suspicion of murder. Said I stabbed a fellow to death in the fight at the Wild Horse. They brought me here, and I been here since."

"Any idea why they think it was you that stabbed the man?" asked Barlow.

Nodding, Earl replied, "Yeah, I got a right purty knife my daddy give me for my birthday last year. It has pearl handles and daddy had my initials engraved on it. One deputy said they found my knife buried in the dead man's heart."

Barlow felt a wave of disappointment. This news was devastating and Earl's father, Robert, would be crushed. "Do you know the dead man?"

"I don't even know who was killed, but Mr. Barlow, I seen your face when I told you about the knife. I didn't stab nobody. Fact is, I keep the knife in my saddlebags, wrapped in an old kerchief. I weren't carrying it. If it's my knife, somebody stole it and used it in the fight to kill the fellow."

Barlow thought about it. It was against the law to carry a gun or a knife but most men carried one or both, carefully hidden, of course. While it was possible someone had stolen the knife and then used it in the fight, it wouldn't sound creditable to a jury. "When was the last time you saw your knife?"

Earl ran his hand through his hair and thought about it. "I guess a couple of weeks ago. Me, Ned and Lou went fishing. On the bay side of the island. I cut up some bait fish with it. No, I used it Friday, the day before we went to the Wild Horse, to cut a plug of tobacco."

"How many people knew you owned the knife?"

Earl shrugged. "I showed it off from time to time."

CHAPTER 4

Robert Crenshaw sat in Barlow's office, listening, his face grim. "I appreciate you convincing the judge to set bail," said Crenshaw. "Earl says he never carried his knife on his person and I believe him, but the idea of someone stealing his knife and… it's just too odd to grasp."

"Did you see the knife? The one that was used?"

"Yes, there is no doubt. It's the one I gave Earl."

"Robert, the one thing that strikes me is, well, just what you said. The thing is odd. The deputy that went out to the Wild Horse said the bartender told him Earl returned to the bar and finished his beer after the fight. If Earl did stabbed the man, I don't think he would have left his knife sticking in him and returned to the bar. Anyway, my investigators will know more in a few days. They're working on another pressing issue, but between us, we'll dig into the situation. The district attorney isn't pressing for a quick trial, so we have some time."

Standing, Crenshaw leaned over the desk, stretched out his hand and shook Barlow's. Barlow walked Crenshaw out and nodded to a man who was waiting to see him. After showing Robert Crenshaw out, Barlow stopped at Phoebe's desk, where she was studying a case law book.

"Did Tobias say anything last night about the Wardlow investigation?"

Looking up, Phoebe replied, "I didn't see him, but he left a note. It said that he and Nathan were headed to Clear Creek."

Barlow nodded. *Looks like the boys are on the trail*, he thought.

Having seen everyone with an appointment, Barlow left the office just after four and hailed a buggy driver for hire. He had the man take him out to the Wild Horse Saloon and asked him to wait. Although it was early, after his eyes adjusted to the dark, he could see a half-dozen men. Two were at the bar and the other four sat at a table with a lamp in the center. A woman was standing close to one of the men at the bar. In a moment, the man and woman turned and headed up the stairs at the back of the room.

At the bar, Barlow ordered a beer. As the bartender set it in front of him, Barlow said, "My name is Barlow."

The bartender, a tall man, hatless and bald, looked at Barlow with a face disfigured by fire. *It was likely the result of a cigarette and a powder horn during the war, given it was on one side of his face,* thought Barlow.

"There'll be another girl down in a bit," said the bartender. "The beer is five cents."

Barlow laid a coin on the bar and said, "I'm not here for a girl. I'd like to hear about the fight last week."

"Talk to the sheriff. He's looking into it. You related to the dead man?"

Barlow shook his head. "I'm a lawyer. You working that night?"

"Yeah, what about it?"

Laying a dollar coin on the bar, Barlow asked, "Mind telling me how it went?"

Shrugging, the bartender picked up the dollar. "Ain't much to tell. It was late. We was busy. When it gets late everybody is drunk, of course, and that's when the trouble starts. Two Germans were the spark, I think. They was here at the bar. Standing right beside the guy, what did the killing. They got to arguing, real loud in German. Then one of them throws a punch, and all hell broke loose."

"How did you know the men were speaking German?" asked Barlow.

"You from around here? Seems like half the population is German."

Barlow nodded. "How do you know the man that did the killing was at the bar?"

"Oh, well, he disappeared off into the brawl. I fired a shotgun through that window there," he pointed to a window at the end of the bar. "That brought things to a halt. So, this fellow that had been right about where you're standing, drinking beer, he steps back up and finishes his beer. He had blood on his shirt, so I knowed he was in the thick of it. But the next day, Frankton, he's the deputy come out here when we found the dead man, he came back out and asked me about the man at the bar. Said his name was, let me see, Crenshaw. Wanted to know what he done and all. Told me he was the one what stabbed the fellow."

"Did you know the man that was killed?" asked Barlow.

"Sure did. He was a regular here on Saturdays. Had a thing for one of the girls. You lawyers all hold yourselves out as special, but you're just like everybody else."

"He was a lawyer?"

Grinning, the bartender replied, "Yep. A. L Haddon."

Barlow nodded. "Fights common here?"

The bartender laughed. "We're a saloon. Of course, fights is common."

Barlow was late arriving back at the hotel. Sadie wasn't in the rooms, but he found her having coffee in the dining room. She didn't smile when he sat down.

"Sorry I'm late," said Barlow.

"Sam, you're not late. Late is ten minutes. You missed supper. It would have been nice if you'd sent me a note. I must insist that you install a telephone at your office so I can call you from the hotel or you can phone the hotel and leave me a message."

Barlow had never been married and never had what could be called a long-term relationship. He had been his own man for so long he was having trouble processing what Sadie was saying. When he didn't respond, Sadie continued, "Sam, I know marriage is new to you, but we're partners now. We're one. It's important we think about each other." She smiled.

"Of course," he replied, thinking there might be more to this marriage thing than he had thought.

CHAPTER 5

Monday afternoon, Tobias and Nathan had packed light bags and caught the noon Galveston, Houston and Henderson train, getting off at the Clear Creek Depot.

"You bring a pistol?" Tobias asked Nathan.

"In my bag," said Nathan. "You?"

Tobias nodded and replied, "I got one in my boot."

Standing on the loading dock in Clear Creek, Tobias and Nathan looked around, but there wasn't much to see. There appeared to be two or three streets and a few buildings along what could be called the main street. Several wagons were there to meet the train, to load and unload freight. A few passengers disembarked with Tobias and Nathan, while a half-dozen waited to board. Both men held small cloth bags as they studied the area.

"What now?" asked Nathan.

"What say we see about some horses and rigs?" said Tobias, pointing to a building in the distance that featured a sign that said Livery & Wagon Yard on it.

An hour later, the two men were mounted, although the horses and saddles were old.

"Well, I reckon the church is the place to start," said Tobias, "but I could use a drink. I'll ask the station master." Returning, a few minutes later, Tobias, grinning, said, "We're in luck."

Shortly, the two men were at the bar in a small saloon, their horses tied to a tree next to the building.

"What'll it be gentlemen?" asked the bartender.

"Beer," said Tobias.

"Same," said Nathan.

The bartender sat two glasses of warm beer in front of the men. As they waited for their eyes to adjust to the darkness, they sipped their drinks. Casually, they studied the near empty room. When the bartender asked them if they wanted another, they both nodded and when he sat them in front of them, Tobias said, "We're looking for a friend. Name of Smith."

The bartender shook his head. "Don't know him. He working at the brick plant? It's south of here. Try there."

"We heard his sister come to live with him," said Tobias.

The bartender frowned. "Can't help you."

The Baptist church was easy to find, its steeple the tallest thing in the area.

The church door was open, but Tobias and Nathan couldn't find anyone about. They exited a rear door into a garden and saw a woman sitting on the ground, working a tool into the soil.

"Good afternoon," said Tobias.

Looking up, the woman said, "Good afternoon, gentlemen," as she rose.

Removing her gloves, she held out a hand. "I'm Mrs. Sims, the pastor's wife. He's at the farm.

Turning her head to look at her garden, she continued, "I've got some winter greens growing."

After shaking hands, Tobias and Nathan introduced themselves. Tobias said, "Nice to meet you. We're here on behalf of the Wardlows."

"Oh my! What has happened?" exclaimed Mrs. Sims.

"They're fine," replied Tobias quickly. "The elder Wardlow's haven't heard from DeWayne and they are concerned. We offered to come by and see if the pastor had seen him or perhaps his wife, Lavinia."

Frowning, Mrs. Sims said, "Well, let me think. They weren't here last Sunday, but I'm not sure about the week before. Pastor Sims might have talked to them, but he hasn't mentioned it. Have you stopped by their home?"

"Actually, we're not sure where it is," replied Nathan.

Mrs. Sims looked at the two of them with a bit of suspicion.

Quickly, Tobias added, "The Wardlows said they never visited DeWayne and Lavinia at their home."

Mrs. Sims seemed to relax. "Likely not, it was love at first sight for those two. The courtship was rather short." She laughed. "Such a sweet girl. I am happy for DeWayne. He's such a quiet young man, I thought he might never find anyone. But no, I'm not sure where they are living."

"You think the Pastor might know where they're staying?" asked Tobias.

"He might. If they're living in town, well, you've seen how small the town is. Pastor Sims will be coming back late. Why don't you stop by tomorrow?"

"We didn't see a hotel," answered Tobias.

"There's a boarding house. Some men that work at the brick plant stay there, but they usually have a room or two available," replied Mrs. Sims. "It's just north of the train station and they serve supper."

Tobias and Nathan thanked her and said their goodbyes.

The two men found the boarding house, an old two-story house.

"Supper is at six, breakfast at five. We don't serve no dinner and you'll have to leave your horses at the livery," stated the boarding house owner.

The next morning, after a breakfast of hot cakes and fried potatoes, Tobias and Nathan walked to the livery and saddled their horses. They arrived at the brick plant just after six in the morning and the place was humming with activity. They tethered their horses with a dozen others in a field with a small watering hole a hundred yards from the plant and they left their mounts before finding a door with 'Office' painted above it. Inside a man sitting at an old desk piled with papers, smoking a huge cigar greeted them.

"We ain't hiring," exclaimed the man, without looking up.

"Good morning," said Tobias. "We was looking for a fellow. Thought maybe he was working here."

"Can't help you," said the man, still studying a paper on his desk.

"His name is Smith," replied Tobias, not deterred.

The man's head shot up. "Smith, you say?"

Surprised at the sudden change in the man's attitude, Tobias replied, "Yes sir."

The man's eyes squinted. "Foreign fellow? Speaks with an accent?"

"That's likely him," said Tobias.

Suddenly the man's hand appeared above the desk, holding a Peacemaker revolver.

Tobias and Nathan stared at the revolver pointing at them.

"Billy! Come in here," yelled the plant manager, without taking his eyes or his gun off of Tobias and Nathan.

22

A burly man opened a door and entered the office, taking in the scene. "What the hell?"

"These fellows are friends with Smith," said the plant manager, not taking his eyes off Tobias and Nathan; the gun held steady.

"No, no, we've never met the man. We're looking for his sister and thought he might tell us where she is," exclaimed Tobias.

No one spoke for several seconds, then the manager asked, "Why are you looking for his sister?"

"We were hired to find a fellow who recently married Smith's sister and we can't find him, so we thought we'd ask Smith about his sister," replied Tobias.

The manager slowly lowered the revolver. "We had a fellow called himself Smith working here, but he's gone and it ain't likely he's going to show his face around here again. Worked here for a week. Sold me a horse and didn't show up for work the next day. Turns out the horse was stolen."

Tobias and Nathan looked at each other.

CHAPTER 6

Twenty miles away, in Galveston, Barlow sat at his desk thinking through the Earl Crenshaw situation. The boy's life was at stake and his father was sick with worry. Barlow felt Earl was telling the truth, but it seemed too coincidental that someone would steal Earl's knife and kill someone with it in a fight that involved Earl. Starting with the premise that it wasn't coincidental, Barlow considered the implications.

Was it possible that someone planned to kill the lawyer, A.L. Haddon, and framed Earl Crenshaw for the murder? Too complicated, thought Barlow. *If someone had a grudge against Earl, they would have killed him rather than frame him for killing someone else. The only possibility Barlow could see was to argue it wasn't Crenshaw who stabbed the man – although his knife was used. Could he convince a jury? Not likely,* he thought.

Barlow looked up to see Phoebe standing in his doorway. "Problem?" he asked.

"Two men are here. Claim they were sent by the telephone company to install a telephone line," said Phoebe, her voice flat, calm.

Barlow sighed, "Sorry, I forgot to talk to you about that. Yes, please have them put a phone somewhere."

Phoebe stared at him. Her face expectant.

"I know I said we couldn't get one because of the confidentially of our work, but Sadie insists I have one so we can communicate."

Phoebe didn't respond. She stood motionless for ten seconds, appeared about to speak, but suddenly turned and left without a word.

Barlow stared after her for a minute as his thoughts returned to the Crenshaw case, he thought, *if only those two Germans hadn't gotten into a fight.* Suddenly he had a new thought. *Was the whole thing planned? Were the Germans part of it?*

Barlow spent the day seeing clients and reviewing two contracts and a will that Phoebe had typed up on the Remington typewriter.

He worked through the noon hour and stepped out of his office at mid-afternoon. He walked over to Phoebe's desk where she was engrossed in a Texas Reports book, which contained Texas Supreme Court rulings. "Phoebe," he said quietly.

Looking up, she said, "What is it Barlow?"

"I'll be leaving at four today. I 'm going back out to the saloon to ask some more questions."

She nodded and went back to her reading. One of Barlow's regular clients, an importer, came in just before four without an appointment and Barlow spent a half hour discussing a problem with him and didn't leave until four-thirty. He was downstairs when he remembered Sadie. He climbed back up the stairs and asked Phoebe to send a boy with a message to the hotel saying he would be late.

"What time shall I say you will arrive home?" asked Phoebe.

"Half-past six," replied Barlow.

Looking at the small wooden box on the wall, Phoebe said, "I'll use the phone. The hotel has a phone, so I can call and give them a message for Sadie."

Frowning, Barlow asked, "Do you know how to use that thing?"

"Yes, Barlow. You turn the little crank on the side. It sends an electric signal to the telephone exchange. When they answer you tell them who you would like to connect with. If the line isn't in use, they will ring your party."

"Fine, but remember, no business talk or mention of where I'm going, you understand."

"I understand," said Phoebe.

Barlow hired a buggy to take him out to the Wild Horse Saloon. Seeing him, the bartender looked unhappy, but Barlow came right to the point. "I'd like you to tell me everything you can remember about the two Germans who started fighting the night A.L. Haddon was killed." The bartender started to say something and Barlow interrupted. "And I don't want to hear you don't remember. Bartenders are very observant and have good memories."

Barlow said it with conviction; the bartender sighed and said, "Yeah, well, you got to keep a keen eye out for trouble and know your customers. One of them comes in now and then. Name is Franz. I don't know his last name. Big fellow. Blonde hair, blue eyes. I heard him tell one of the girls he was strong because he worked as a stevedore."

"The other man involved in the fight?"

"Rough looking dude. Nose has bent, probably broken a few times. Big, but smaller than Franz. Long brown hair. Tattoo of a spider on his right hand."

Barlow slid a dollar onto the bar, "Thanks."

CHAPTER 7

After telling the manager of the brick plant they would be glad to let him know if they ran across Smith while they were looking for his sister, Tobias and Nathan left and returned to the church. They found Pastor Sims arranging hymnals in the church pews. When they explained they were there just to make sure DeWayne Wardlow was well; his parents hadn't heard from him; the pastor smiled.

"Oh, I'd say he's very well. I saw him and Lavinia just yesterday. They are newly wedded you know."

Tobias smiled. "Why that's good news. I reckon he's so busy with his new bride he ain't thought to contact his parents. We'll let them know he's okay. Say, do you know where they're staying? Just in case the parents ask."

"Oh, yes of course. They're in the little yellow house behind the general store. I think Lavinia's brother was staying there, but she said he's moved back to Houston." The pastor's eyes glazed over as if he were deep in thought. "I have always said you can't judge people by the color of their skin or their origins. Lavinia is as sweet a young woman as you'd ever hope to meet."

Tobias and Nathan's faces showed surprise at the pastor's statement.

"Ah, we've never had the chance to meet them. Is Lavinia dark-skinned?" asked Nathan.

The pastor laughed. "No, no, she is dark, but no, not like you're thinking. That wouldn't be legal, you know. It's just that you hear so many bad things about the Roma."

"Beg your pardon," said Tobias, frowning.

"The Gypsies," replied the pastor.

"Can't say I know 'em," said Tobias, looking at Nathan, who shook his head.

The pastor nodded. "They are a minority group from Europe, like so many others. You may have crossed paths with one. The women often work as fortune-tellers."

Both Tobias and Nathan expressed surprise. "Yes sir, I reckon I've seen a fortune-teller or two in San Francisco," said Tobias.

"New Orleans," said Nathan, "but I never heard them referred to as Roma or Gypsies."

"Oh, yes, I've heard the term 'travelers' used with the word 'gypsy'," added Tobias.

Smiling, Pastor Sims replied, "That's common, but the Travelers you refer to are from Ireland and not related to Romany Gypsies." Tobias and Nathan stared at the pastor and he continued. I spent several years traveling in England and Europe."

"Well, okay then. Thank you very much sir, we'll tell Mr. and Mrs. Wardlow all is well," said Tobias and then pulling some coins from his pocket, continued, "we'd like to donate to the church."

By late afternoon, Tobias and Nathan had returned their horses, and were waiting for the train to Galveston, but not before riding by the house where DeWayne and Lavinia were staying. Tobias studied the area so he could write how to find it.

Meanwhile, back at the office, Barlow walked out and spoke to Phoebe.

"Please make a list of our clients who work in import/export or shipping and their addresses. I need Tobias and Nathan to find a couple of stevedores for me."

"Of course," replied Phoebe, when suddenly the room was filled with a loud clanging sound. The two clients waiting, Phoebe and Barlow were all startled and looked around the room for the source of the clanging. Their eyes fell on the wooden box on the wall. The two silver round silver attachments on it were vibrating.

"Can you stop it?" asked Barlow, his voice tense.

Phoebe rose, walked to the phone and lifted the receiver. The clanging stopped. She listened. After a minute she said, "Of course," then replaced the receiver in the hanger on the side of the box. After walking back to her desk where Barlow had remained standing, she said, "Sadie wanted me to let you know she has accepted a dinner invitation for the two of you to dine with the Adlays. It is for tonight at seven at Castille's."

With that, Phoebe took her seat and began working. Barlow stood silent, his face a mask. Finally, he turned and walked back into his office. Just before closing time, Tobias and Nathan came rambling into the office. Phoebe told them to have a seat while she checked with Barlow, who told her to send them in and for her to come as well.

Barlow listened carefully while they briefed him. "Excellent work," he said. "Phoebe, please draft a motion to put the order to vacate on hold until we have a court hearing and a motion to make the deed transfer void. The sheriff can serve notice on Dewayne now that we know where he's staying."

"Can we win in court?" asked Nathan.

"Probably not, but this will buy us some time to figure out our next move," replied Barlow.

"True or not, gypsies have a reputation for being less than honest. I'm sure, among them, there's good and bad just like every other group. Her brother selling a stolen horse sheds a dim light on the family for sure. It's possible that her brother is working with her to steal the Wardlow's ranch, using their son, DeWayne, to do it."

"I'm inclined to believe DeWayne is being duped. He's probably letting his manhood drive his thinking," said Phoebe.

Nathan and Tobias looked at each other and Tobias blushed at his wife's comment.

Barlow smiled. "I concur," he said.

Looking at Tobias and Nathan, Barlow said, "Fact is, you two returned just in time. I need you to find two stevedores for me. They are the ones who started the fight out at the Wild Horse the night A.L. Haddon was murdered. I suspect they were paid to start that fight. Let them know we want nothing except the name of who paid them. Offer them money for the name. Fellows like that are usually loyal to money. Phoebe will give you a list of our clients in the trade, start with them."

Barlow described the two men he was looking for and told the two to start first thing in the morning.

In the small yellow house in Clear Creek, at that very moment, DeWayne Wardlow was sitting at the kitchen table, his face a mask of concern.

"Why is my man's mustache drooping?" asked Lavinia in a slow, sexy voice. She was standing behind him and she put her hands on his shoulders.

"Well, Lavinia, I feel bad you know. Making my folks leave the ranch. It don't seem right."

Leaning down and putting her face close to DeWayne, Lavinia purred, "Baby, we've talked about this. They're too old to take care of a ranch. We're going to find them a fine home in town. They'll be so happy once they're there and they see how nice it is."

"I know you're right; I just hate they're gonna be mad at me and all."

"That won't last a whole day, sweetheart. Just you wait and see," replied Lavinia. "We're going to use some of the money from the sale of the ranch to get them a nice house and new furniture and whatever they want."

DeWayne smiled a weak smile.

"Remember, we prayed about it and the Lord spoke to us. It is the right thing to do."

DeWayne smiled and replied, "I know you're right about pa and ma. It's like you said the other day. I'm used to them telling me what to do, and it's time I took charge and looked after them."

You're making me frisky," purred Lavinia. "What say we take a nap?"

CHAPTER 8

Mary Beth's face turned hard when she saw Tobias and Phoebe arrive at their house, arm in arm. She had been waiting across the street, convincing herself Tobias would come calling on her as soon as he was back in Galveston from where ever he was. She returned home, seething with anger.

Earl Crenshaw and the murder charge against him filled Barlow's thoughts most of his waking hours, but the Adlays were always good company. Barlow was enjoying visiting with them and spending time with Sadie as they ate a fine meal at Castile's Restaurant. The king mackerel was fresh and delicious. Peter Adlay was a banker and a well-read man. He was always current on the political situation.

"Peter, James Garfield will be sworn in as president in March. What are your thoughts? I know little about the man," said Barlow.

Peter Adlay smiled. This was his area of interest. "Republican, attorney, so far only sitting member of the House to be elected to the Presidency. Served in the War. Favors the gold standard. I don't think we'll see any radical differences between his service and that of Hayes."

Peter's wife, Clarissa asked, "I keep hearing about the gold standard. Whatever does that mean, Peter?"

"It means the United States Government has to back all the paper money it issues with gold," he explained.

"I see," said Clarissa and she and Sadie began talking to each other.

Barlow heard Sadie say, "I've found the perfect house. Three stories with windows facing the ocean breezes. However, the best part is it has a grand room on the first floor that will be perfect for entertaining."

This was news to Barlow, who was perfectly happy living at the hotel and who had no plans to entertain anyone. He realized Peter was talking to him. "I'm sorry, didn't catch that."

31

"Oh, I was just saying the railroads are going to change the face of Texas in the next decade. We can expect new towns and industries as they expand. For example, the town lots for that place in West Texas, Abilene, it's being called, go on sale in a few months and according to the newspapers, there are already hundreds of people camping out there, waiting."

Barlow smiled, and Peter continued talking as he ate, expanding on the building of the railroad across the country to California, but Barlow's thoughts were returning to Earl Crenshaw and the mystery of what happened in the Wild Horse Saloon. Sadie was quiet as they rode in a hired buggy back to their rooms at the hotel and Barlow continued to consider his investigation into the murder of A.L. Haddon, for which his client, Earl Crenshaw had been charged.

Once in their rooms, Sadie said, "Sam, I enjoyed the evening and I thank you for it, but you seemed preoccupied."

"I did? As I told you, I'm defending a young man on a murder charge and cases like this consume one's thoughts."

"It's admirable that you take it so serious and I would expect no less of you, but really, Sam. You're not at work. Surely you can do your research and plan your strategy at the office. In fact, I've been meaning to speak to you. I see so very little of you. You're always home late, you never ask me to join you for the noon meal and when you are here, you're lost in thought."

Smiling a wry smile, Barlow replied, "It's not always like this, but when a man's life is at stake, not to mention his family's pain and distress, I have to concentrate on his situation. As his attorney, I've taken on the responsibility for his life; I've become him, in a manner."

Her lips set in a grim line, Sadie responded, "I can understand that and given that is how you feel, I believe you're going to have to consider restricting your practice to contracts and such. You will have regular hours and we can spend more time doing things together. Things we enjoy, like the theatre. Sam, you've forgotten how to enjoy life." She stared at him for a moment. When he didn't respond, she continued, "Why don't you sleep in your room tonight?"

CHAPTER 9

When Tobias and Phoebe stepped out of their house on Wednesday morning, laughing, Mary Beth watched from across the street. She had climbed out of her bedroom window, early that morning. Her face turned hard and red. So, it was true. The cad had married this, this, woman. On her way home, Mary Beth stopped by the church and working quickly, digging through the donation basket of clothing, found a hat, shawl and dress that would fit her. They were all old and worn, but clean. After looking around, to make sure no one had seen her, she tucked her items under her arm and hurried home.

Tobias and Phoebe found Nathan waiting when they arrived at the bank building. The Barlow law office was on the second floor.

"Good morning Nathan. How is Elvira?" asked Phoebe.

"She's well, thank you," replied Nathan.

Phoebe squeezed Tobias's arm and headed up the stairs.

"Looks like things are going well for you," said Nathan, smiling.

"Tis, how about you?" asked Tobias.

"It's requiring a bit of adjusting, but I'm happy, Tobias. I wonder every day how I got so lucky."

Tobias and Nathan stepped off, headed for the waterfront to visit the offices of the shipping companies asking about the man with the spider tattoo on his hand and the big, blonde man, Franz. They had no luck that morning and visited one more company before having dinner. The receptionist listened to their request to see her boss and told them he was in New Orleans.

"Well, we was trying to locate a couple of gents that's working as stevedores, thought he might know them," explained Tobias, disappointed.

"Oh, well, he wouldn't be much help," she said, laughing. "You two need to see Franklin Alcott, down at the docks. He runs things down there. He'll know them if they work around the ships."

Franklin Alcott didn't have to think. "Yep, I know 'em. You'll find them loading the St. Martin, two piers to the west. Franz and Koch. Find one and the other will be close by."

Tobias offered him a dollar gold piece, but Alcott shook his head, and without a word turned away and began shouting orders at a group standing around a stack of wooden crates.

A few minutes later, Nathan and Tobias were watching the St. Martin being loaded. Thirty or forty men were hard at work. The two waited until the foreman called for a break and the men broke into small groups, and began smoking, and talking as they drank water from dippers hanging from barrels filled with water. Walking among the groups they spotted the tall blonde German, Franz, and approached him.

"Can we have a word?" asked Tobias.

The man stared at him. Frowning, the man looked at the man beside him, who lifted a cigarette to his lips with a hand that sported a tattoo of a spider.

"Why don't the two of you give us a minute of your time. It might be profitable to you?"

The smaller man with the spider tattoo, Koch, shrugged and the four men walked away from the group. "My boss here will pay for some information," stated Tobias, looking over at Nathan.

The big German frowned. "What kind of information?" he asked.

Smiling, Tobias said, "We know you and your friend here were paid to fight out at the Wild Horse." The man started to interrupt, but Tobias held up his hand. "There's lots of fights. My boss here couldn't care less about you two. What he wants to know, is who paid you. We ain't planning to tell anybody how we know, so there's no worry there."

The big, blonde man looked at Nathan who was holding up a ten-dollar gold piece. The man looked over at his partner, who was licking his lips.

"Break time is almost up. So is the offer," said Tobias.

"Fellow name of Spidley. He's around the Wild Horse some. Everybody calls him Mad Dog, on account of he served five years up to the prison in Huntsville and it done something to him. He's a hard case. I wouldn't fool with him, was I you'uns," said the man with the spider tattoo, who held out his hand. Nathan placed the coin in the man's hand and he and Tobias turned and walked away.

As they walked back to work, the big blonde man looked at his partner and asked, "Why did you tell him it was Mad Dog? He's liable to come looking for us. Couldn't you think of nobody else?"

"His name just popped in my head. I seen him playing poker the night we started the fight."

"They figure out we was lying; they'll want their ten dollars back."

Barlow listened carefully to Tobias as he explained the results of their visit to the waterfront. "I think you boys may have saved Earl Crenshaw, but we'll need more. Visit the courthouse and look at the court record on Spidley. See what he was convicted of. And see if anyone knows how he makes his living," said Barlow.

"Will do," said Tobias and Nathan nodded.

"Nathan, a constable is going to serve DeWayne Wardlow today with notice that there will be a hearing next week regarding the order to force his parents from their home. The constable plans to take the train this afternoon. I'd like you to go up there and stay. Keep an eye on the house. After the constable serves him I want you to follow him and Lavinia if they leave. Phoebe, send a copy of the summons by messenger to the attorney in Houston who handled the eviction notice and change of deed for DeWayne. Tobias, I need you to stay here and help me on the Earl Crenshaw murder case."

"Sir, what if only one of them leaves the house, or they split up?" asked Nathan.

Barlow considered for a moment and replied, "Follow Lavinia. Buy a train ticket to Houston and one back to Galveston. If they get on either train, you'll be ready to board without calling attention to yourself."

Nathan left and went home to pack a bag and catch the train. Tobias, fully aware that as far as Phoebe was concerned, when they were at work, they were simply co-workers, so he stopped by her desk only long enough to tell her he was going to the courthouse. She nodded and went back to the papers she was working on.

At the courthouse Tobias found the court results on Spidley's trial. The man had been found guilty of attempted murder. He had slashed and stabbed a man during a card game. No one at the courthouse knew anything else about Spidley, so Tobias walked to the sheriff's office to ask him.

"Spidley, you say?" said the sheriff, looking thoughtful.

"Some folks call him Mad Dog," said Tobias.

The sheriff laughed. "Oh, Mad Dog, sure I know Mad Dog. He's a regular guest here at the jail."

"Any idea how he supports himself?"

"When he isn't in jail, he loads wagons for a freighter name of Jones. If Jones is off on a trip, he helps at the livery on fourth street. Seems he's pretty good with animals and fixing wagons."

"He usually in here for drinking?" asked Tobias.

"Nope. The man suffers from sort of constant suspicion. Gets to thinking people are looking at him, talking about him. Told me more than once somebody or other was thinking to kill him. Disorderly conduct, fighting, that sort of thing. I reckon that's how the handle 'Mad Dog' caught on. He's smart enough and all. Just has this thing in his head."

"Appreciate it, sheriff," said Tobias.

Arriving back at the office, Tobias filled Barlow in on what he had learned.

Barlow listened and sat, silently thinking. Finally, he said, "It would appear that this fellow, Mad Dog, planned this murder, but somehow it doesn't seem to fit what we know about him. Using a knife, yes, but given his history, I don't see him planning a murder. Seems like he acts on impulse. Tobias, visit Doc Evans. Ask him about this type behavior."

Back at home, Mary Beth's mother asked her to accompany her on a shopping trip, but Mary Beth demurred, saying she thought it best if she rested. As soon as her mother left, Mary Beth found a jar of apple preserves and began making the crust for an apple pie. It would be a special pie. It would have one key ingredient. Arsenic. There was a can in the back of the cupboard. It was used regularly to kill rats. She had been told as a child that it had no smell or taste and had to be carefully labeled and kept from small children as it was a deadly poison.

When the pie was done, Mary Beth set it on the window sill to cool. She found a cotton flour sack; her mother saved them for wiping the dishes dry. When the pie was cool, she wrapped the sack around it. Her mother would be gone another hour or two, but Mary Beth hurriedly changed into the donated clothing she had taken from the charity box at the church, picked up the pie and headed for Tobias and Phoebe's house. There, after making sure no one was around, she left the pie on the doorstep. She knew Tobias. He would never pass up an apple pie. She smiled.

Tobias hadn't returned from his visit to see Dr. Evans when Phoebe closed up the office for the night. She was taken aback when she saw the flour sack covered pie on the doorstep. She picked it up. No note. She looked around to see if a note might have blown away, but didn't see one. She entered the house and set the pie on the kitchen table. She expected Tobias soon, so she set about starting a fire in the stove to warm the house and prepare supper. The pie was still on her mind and she took the flour sack and looked inside it for a note, but found nothing. She was puzzled.

After putting some water on the wood stove to boil, she sat down and studied the pie. Using a spoon, she carefully parted some of the crust and looked at the filling. Apple. Tobias's favorite. She was curious about the source of the pie. It was likely someone would mention it in a day or two; ask if they enjoyed it. She was what? Irked? She wasn't sure, but years with Barlow had taught her some thinking skills.

It is a homemade apple pie.
Women make pies.
A woman made this pie.
It is an apple pie.
Apple is Tobias's favorite.
This pie is for Tobias.
A woman made this pie for Tobias.
The woman did not leave a note.
This woman did not want me to know who made it.
Tobias won't care. As soon as he finishes supper, he will eat a large piece or maybe two.

She reached over, wrapped the pie in the flour sack, stood, picked up the pie and hid it on the top shelf of the cabinet. "It'll keep for a few days," she said out loud.

CHAPTER 10

Nathan had been on the same train as the constable, but didn't speak to him. Per Barlow's instructions, he had purchased a ticket to Houston and one back to Galveston. The stationmaster looked at him, but didn't comment. Tobias followed the constable to the yellow house where DeWayne Wardlow and his new wife, Lavinia, were staying. Lingering across the street, Nathan got his first look at DeWayne, who opened the door and stepped outside. The constable spoke to him and handed him a folded paper. DeWayne opened it and read it. The constable turned and hurried back to the train station, hoping to catch the train before it left. DeWayne went inside. Nathan watched. After an hour, the train had certainly departed, and no one had come out of the house. He walked to the boardinghouse he and Tobias had stayed at on their previous visit and took a room, but dawn found him outside the yellow house.

Nathan had eaten quickly at the boardinghouse before making his way back to his spot across the street from the yellow house. The first train came through at ten o'clock.

Inside the house, the atmosphere was tense. DeWayne had been terribly upset the day before when the notice of a court hearing regarding the order for his parents to vacate their home had been served on DeWayne. Lavinia had been calm and cool, but it had shaken DeWayne.

"Will they be there? In court?" DeWayne had demanded. "I can't face them."

Lavinia reassured him and told him he needed to go to Houston to see the lawyer and tell him about the hearing.

"Yes, we'll need him there," said DeWayne.

Lavinia hesitated and then replied, "Perhaps I can do some shopping while you see the lawyer."

"Why sure," said DeWayne.

"Wonderful. You go see the lawyer and I will shop and meet you back here tonight."

DeWayne frowned.

"I don't think you want to follow me around for hours while I look at material," continued Lavinia. "What say, we meet up at the train station and catch the four o'clock back to Cedar Springs."

DeWayne smiled and nodded his agreement.

Nathan watched as DeWayne and a dark haired and dark-complexed woman left the house and walked toward the train station. On the train, Nathan sat on the bench behind the two. Their conversation wasn't helpful other than to discover that DeWayne was going to see his lawyer and Lavinia was planning to do some shopping. *Lavinia was pretty,* thought Nathan, *but how had she convinced DeWayne to put his parents out of their own home?*

In Houston, Dewayne and Lavinia walked in different directions and Nathan followed Lavinia as he had been instructed to do by Barlow. She stepped into a rented buggy near the train station and Nathan did the same, instructing the driver to follow the other buggy. The man did so without comment. His passenger might be following his wife and he would not put his nose in someone else's affairs.

Nathan was completely taken aback when Lavinia stepped down from her buggy in Happy Hollow. An area of Houston known for its brothels, saloons, gambling and crime. She walked purposely and entered a saloon. Nathan followed her. Inside, he hesitated, to let his eyes adjust to the darkness, but when they did, he saw Lavinia held tightly by a long-haired man, who was kissing her forcefully.

Nathan stepped up to the bar and ordered a beer. After a few minutes, Lavinia and the man left, arm in arm and Nathan followed them outside. They went down the street and entered a run-down hotel. Nathan followed them in. They didn't stop at the counter, but went up the stairs. Unsure what to do, Nathan went to the counter and asked for a room.

After paying the clerk, Nathan said, "I'm meeting a friend. Okay, I wait here? I'll get the key later," he asked pointing to the only chair in the tiny lobby.

"Suit yourself," replied the clerk.

Nathan sat, tilted his hat over his face and waited. They didn't come down until two hours later.

When they left, Nathan stood, stretched and followed them back to the saloon where they had met. Finding himself waiting at the bar, yet again, Nathan ordered a beer and two boiled eggs.

The bartender, noticing him casting furtive glances at the couple, leaned over the bar and said, "Forget it friend. She don't work here no more."

Surprise registered on Nathan's face and the bartender grinned. Pleased he had shocked this cowboy.

Sensing he was on to something, Nathan said, "Oh I ain't never been here, but she's purty."

"You'd be best advised to mind your own business. She used to work here as a saloon girl. No funny business you understand; she would talk to you and maybe dance with you for a dollar or two, long as you was buying drinks, and the owner paid her for doing it. One night a fellow got drunk and a little too friendly. The fellow she's with, her husband, Vano Smith, cut the fellow up pretty badly."

"I don't need no trouble. Reckon I'll drink somewhere else if it's all the same to you," said Nathan, "but thanks for the information." After laying a dollar on the counter for the bartender, Nathan finished his beer and walked out.

He waited across the street until Lavinia came out and then followed her to the train station where DeWayne was waiting. The three boarded the train. DeWayne and Lavinia got off in Clear Creek, but Nathan rode back to Galveston.

Tobias had gone outback to visit the outhouse and when he came back in, he said, "I found a dead rat right outside our back door. Weren't that big, but I hate rats. Somebody must have put out some poison." Phoebe stared at him. "You all right?" he asked.

"I'm fine," she said, smiling.

"Well, I'm glad I found the rat afore the cats did. If they had eaten it, could a killed them I guess. I've got to go, Dr. Evans weren't in yesterday and I got to see him afore I go to the office," said Tobias. He leaned over and kissed Phoebe, grabbed his hat hanging on the nail by the door and left.

After a minute, Phoebe put a chair close to the cabinet and stood on it so she could see the apple pie she had secreted there. The flour sack had been disturbed. She grabbed the pie and stepped down off the chair, placing the pie on the table. No doubt. A rat had been at the pie. *The same rat?* She wondered.

Finding Dr. Evans in his office and available, Tobias explained about Mad Dog's constant suspicion and thoughts that people were talking about him.

"How interesting," said Dr. Evans. "There is a name for what you are describing. Paranoia. I'm not an expert. I can refer you to an alienist although most neurologists consider mental disorders their field since it involves the brain."

"Alienist," stated Tobias.

"Oh, a doctor of the mind, you know, a doctor who treats insane persons. A neurologist is simply a doctor who specializes in injuries to the brain."

"Does this paranoia keep you from thinking straight, like you're drunk?" asked Tobias.

"No, not like that. It's more like you have thoughts that aren't true, but the person suffering from paranoia thinks they are true. They might, for example, see you talking to someone and believe passionately that you are not only talking about them, but mean them harm."

"Are they dangerous, these folks?"

"They can be. Often they physically confront people."

"Well, all right then, doctor. Thank you. Mr. Barlow said to send your bill to his office. If he thinks we need to talk to one of them alien doctors I'll come by," said Tobias.

That evening, Phoebe showed Tobias the pie and explained it had been left on the stoop without a note. Tobias didn't question her about why she hadn't served it the night before; he was too alarmed.

"You reckon it has poison in it?" he asked.

"I think it might," replied Phoebe. Then she told him about the visit by the woman who introduced herself as Mary Beth. Tobias looked stunned.

"Mary Beth. We went out a few times, but it weren't nothing serious. No, it couldn't a been her."

CHAPTER 11

Friday morning, Barlow called Phoebe, Tobias and Nathan into his office and everyone sat at the large table.

"Let's all discuss where we are on our two pending court cases," said Barlow, who looked tired and haggard. "First, Earl Crenshaw. Charged with the murder of attorney A.L. Haddon, by stabbing. Haddon was killed in a brawl at the Wild Horse Saloon. A fancy knife, which Earl admits was his, was the weapon used to kill Haddon. However, Earl swears he did not stab Haddon. Tobias."

"Ah, well, me and Nathan discovered that the two fellows at the bar standing beside Earl Crenshaw, were the ones that sparked the brawl, but they stated they were paid to start a fight with each other. According to them two, a fellow by the name of Spidley, known as Mad Dog paid them to do it."

"What do we know about this Mad Dog character?" asked Barlow, for the benefit of everyone.

"Ah, he served five years in Huntsville for attempted murder; with a knife. Folks say he suffers from delusions. He thinks people are talking about him and maybe trying to kill him. Dr. Evans says it's a mental thing, called 'paranoia' and folks suffering from it can be violent."

A moment passed while everyone thought about what they had heard. "Do people who suffer from this mental problem plan out attacks or they do it sudden like?" asked Phoebe.

"That is something we need to study on," replied Barlow. "Tobias, you and Nathan go out to the Wild Horse and ask the bartender if Spidley was there the night of the murder and where he was sitting. He'll talk for a dollar or two. I'm going to talk to Earl again about his knife. Phoebe, see what you can find out about the possibility of someone suffering from paranoia planning an attack. You might start with Dr. Evans." Everyone was silent as Barlow seemed to think. "Phoebe, another thing. See if you can find out who Haddon might have represented in the past. A case with a bad outcome, perhaps. He's got a law partner. Now, some things he can't tell you, but explain how important it is he tell us what he can. Anything else on Crenshaw?"

When no one spoke, Barlow said, "Let's move onto the Wardlow situation. They signed the deed to their ranch over to their son, DeWayne after he and his new wife Lavinia encouraged them to. The idea was it would prevent any issues of ownership when they passed. There was a verbal agreement that Eb and Geneva, the owners of the ranch, DeWayne's parents, would continue to live there and work the ranch as usual until they died. Dewayne has not been in contact with his parents, but they have received an order from the Justice of the Peace to vacate within thirty days. Phoebe."

"We have moved to suspend the thirty day vacate notice and a suit challenging the assignment of the deed. DeWayne was served yesterday and his attorney was provided a copy of the motion by messenger, also yesterday. The hearing is next Thursday."

"Thank you Phoebe. Nathan," said Barlow.

"Yes sir. It appears DeWayne's wife, Lavinia may have been married to a man named Vano Smith when she married DeWayne and in fact, is still married to him. Also, Mr. Smith is accused by the manager of the brick plant in Clear Creek of selling him a stolen horse."

"Nathan, send a telegram to Clyde at Dependable Investigations in Austin. Ask him to have someone check marriage records at ports, starting with New York. See if he can find something on Vano Smith. If he's not successful, we'll need him to check other ports, including Galveston. You and Tobias put your heads together and figure out a way to lure Mr. Smith back to Clear Creek and a way to have him arrested for selling a stolen horse. Once he's in jail in Galveston County, I'll see if I can convince the judge to deny bail. If he's in jail, we'll have access to him. Anything else?"

No one spoke and Barlow continued, "Everyone is doing good work. What say we all meet back here this evening at five o'clock. Any objections?"

Everyone stood and left, but Phoebe stepped back in the office and asked, "Barlow, can I speak to you for a minute?"

Barlow nodded and Phoebe closed the door. She told him about the pie. Barlow frowned.

"If it is poisoned, we have a serious problem," said Barlow. "Do you still have the pie?"

"Yes," replied Phoebe.

"Take it with you when you go to see Doctor Evans. Explain what happened to him."

"You look a bit tired," said Phoebe.

"Oh, my routine has been disrupted a bit by married life," replied Barlow, smiling.

Phoebe nodded, but she knew something much more than the disruption of his routine, was troubling Barlow. He always felt pressure when someone's life depended on him, but something else was going on. Only one thing had changed. He had married.

"Why don't you go home and pick up your pie and see Dr. Evans. Ask him if a person with paranoia would plan an attack while you're there. When you finish, see Haddon's law partner. I'll handle the office until you return."

CHAPTER 12

Nathan and Tobias stopped at the telegraph office and sent a telegram to Clyde at Dependable Investigations in Austin, asking him to check marriage records, beginning in New York. It was now mid-morning, and they stopped for coffee to discuss how to get Vano Smith back to Clear Creek, before they went out to the Wild Horse to brace the bartender. Sitting in the Island Café, sipping coffee and smoking, the two men looked at each other.

Finally, Tobias spoke. "I reckon we do what we have to do to see Mr. Vano Smith gets his day in court on this horse stealing thing."

Nathan smiled. "I know where he's staying. How about we send him a telegram and say it's from Lavinia and it's important he meet her in Clear Creek. Then we tell the brick plant manager he's likely to be arriving on the train. Give him time to get a deputy up there."

"Why, I hope you didn't strain your head thinking that up. One hell of a good idea," announced Tobias, grinning. "What say we finish our smokes and coffee and head out to the Wild Horse?"

The bartender was busy preparing for the day. Tobias and Nathan found him in the stockroom.

"We'd have a word," said Tobias.

The bartender looked over at him and said, "I'm busy."

Tobias stood there, filling the doorway, staring at the man, his face hard. The bartender sighed.

"What do you want?" he asked.

"Why don't we have a seat out front?" said Tobias. "We're here on a business matter."

With that, the bartender's attitude changed. "All right then."

The bartender drew three beers, and the men sat at a table. "So, what can I do for you?" he asked.

"We're here to discuss the night Mr. Haddon was killed," said Tobias.

The bartender groaned. "I've told the sheriff what happened."

"Sure. We've got some questions and if you are helpful, we're happy to pay for your time. We know a fellow known as Mad Dog frequents this place. Where was he sitting the night of the fight?"

"Mad Dog? He was playing poker with old Bill Perkins."

"Poker?" asked Tobias.

"Yeah, over there in the back corner. There's usually somebody wants to play cards, but Mad Dog is always up for a game. Only problem is, he always going off on folks. I had to tap him on the head with my stick twice just last month."

"Why do you let him in if he's trouble?" asked Nathan.

Smiling, the bartender said, "Why do you think? He drinks right regular."

"He play with Perkins often?" asked Tobias.

"No, no. Mad Dog is pretty good at cards and being as he gets angry a lot, the regulars don't much like to play with him. Perkins is in off and on, more on since his boy died, but that's the first time I seen him play poker."

"How did his boy die?" asked Nathan.

"I heard he was lost at sea in a storm. Old Perkins ain't been the same since. Blames the ship owner for not having safety lines and whatnot. Rants and raves sometimes when he's drunk."

"I hadn't heard. Who owned the ship?" asked Tobias.

"It was in the Galveston News last month. I think the owner was, let me think, oh yeah, Crenshaw, Crenshaw Shipping."

Tobias and Nathan looked at each other. Tobias pulled a large, two-dollar bill from his pocket, unfolded it and laid it on the table. The bartender picked it up and studied it. It was over seven inches long and over three inches wide. It was labeled: United States Note."

"I wonder why they changed these to read United States Note, and not Treasury Note," said the bartender. "Some kind of government ruse I reckon."

"You got me," said Tobias. "They all spend." With that he placed fifteen cents on the table. "For the beers," he said as he and Nathan stood and walked away.

Dr. Evans thought Phoebe had brought him a pie and was very surprised when she told him she suspected it was poisoned.

"Poisoned, you say," said the doctor, staring at the pie that Phoebe was holding.

Reaching out and taking it, the doctor said, "Leave it with me. I will apply my scientific mind to the issue and let you know tomorrow."

"Thank you, and I have a question. I believe Tobias discussed a mental condition called paranoia with you."

"Yes, he did," replied the doctor.

"Regarding that, you said if someone has this condition they can get violent, thinking someone is talking about them or perhaps they are a threat. Is that correct?"

"Yes, yes," said the doctor. "They often resort to violence."

"My question is, might they plan revenge on someone they think is a threat?"

"You mean plan out an attack in advance? Well, I guess they might think about it for a minute or two, but no, not a long-term plan or at least I haven't heard of a situation like that."

"Thank you Dr. Evans. I see you have a telephone. We just had one installed. Perhaps I could call you tomorrow about the pie. Well, it'll be Saturday. Will you be in?"

"Yes, that would be fine, and I'll be here until noon, but I don't think it would be wise to discuss, you know, poisoned pies on the phone. Folks might get all kinds of notions in their head. What say when you call, ask for an appointment and if the pie is not poisoned, I will say, 'Thank you for calling. I'll thank you for the wonderful pie, and I will tell you I am busy. If it is poisoned, I won't mention the pie, just ask you to come in after work."

"Excellent," said Phoebe.

Phoebe's next stop was A.L. Haddon's office, to see his law partner. After introducing herself, Phoebe explained Barlow was representing Earl Crenshaw, they felt Crenshaw was innocent and were interested in finding out if any of A.L. Haddon's former clients might have held a grudge strong enough to kill him.

"Well, that's a thought, but we don't do criminal work. Wills and probate work mostly. We did occasionally handle a civil lawsuit, but I can't think of anyone who made threats."

Returning to the office, Phoebe found the room full and Barlow talking to a client in his office. She stuck her head in his door and Barlow smiled.

"So glad you are back," said Barlow. "When Mr. Smothers and I finish our business I am going to be out of the office for an hour."

"Sure thing, boss," said Phoebe.

Barlow left his office and took a rented buggy down to the waterfront to the office of Crenshaw Shipping. He was quickly shown into Robert Crenshaw's office. Crenshaw jumped up and shook hands with Barlow.

"Any news?" asked Crenshaw, his face reflecting his anxiety.

"We're making progress," said Barlow. "I actually came by to visit with Earl if he's about."

"Of course, of course. Use my office. I'll send him in." With that Robert Crenshaw hurried out and in less than two minutes his son, Earl stepped in.

"Shut the door and have a seat," said Barlow.

After sitting in a chair beside Barlow, Earl asked, "Things looking bad, Mr. Barlow?"

"We're making progress Earl, but I need some more information regarding your knife. You always kept in your saddlebags, wrapped in a kerchief. Is that correct?"

"Yes, sir."

"Now, you told me you showed it around some. Did you take it out to show people often?"

Earl began shaking his head no. "Ah, no, I mean I didn't like take it out to brag and that. I mean if I was using it to cut something or whatnot, and someone said something, I would show it to them."

"I see. Tell me about the friends you were with."

"Yes, sir. Ned Langston and Lou Perkins. Well, me and Ned have run together since we was kids. We met Lou and his brother last summer at a dance and since then they run with us some. But Lou's brother is, well was, a sailor and gone a lot, but he died last month. Fell overboard in a storm. Lou ain't run with us since, well, until the night of the fight. Him and his brother was close."

"That's unfortunate," said Barlow. "Ned and Lou were upstairs with working girls when the fight broke out. Is that correct?"

"Yes, sir."

"Do you know a fellow folks call, Mad Dog?"

"No sir, can't say I do."

"Did you know the man that was killed? A.L. Haddon. He was a lawyer."

"No sir."

"All right Earl, I'll get back to you as soon as I can," said Barlow.

At a little after five o'clock, the last client left the office and Phoebe locked the door. Everyone met once again at the conference table in Barlow's office.

"Phoebe, why don't you lead off," said Barlow.

"Dr. Evans has never heard of a person suffering from paranoia planning an attack."

Barlow nodded. "I think the fellows that told Tobias and Nathan that Mad Dog paid them to start a fight were lying. Probably they know of him and gave his name to get paid."

"Tobias."

"Well sir, me and Nathan went out to see the bartender at the Wild Horse like you said and he was willing to talk. I gave him two dollars for his time and the information."

"Two dollars?" quired Phoebe.

Barlow laughed. "It's okay. Crenshaw is paying all expenses. What did you find out?"

"Mad Dog was there on the night of the murder. He was playing poker with Bill Perkins. Now, the interesting thing is, Perkin's son was working on a ship and fell overboard and died last month. The ship belonged to Crenshaw Shipping."

Barlow's eyes squinted. "Crenshaw Shipping. You sure?"

"The bartender said it was in the Galveston News."

"It must have been while we were all on our honeymoons," said Barlow.

No one spoke. The room remained silent for a minute.

"One of Earl Crenshaw's friends is Lou Perkins. It was his brother on Crenshaw's ship," said Barlow. "Another thing, I'm leaning toward one of Earl's friends, either Lou or Ned as being the one that stole his knife. They were upstairs when the fight took place, but one of them might have stolen the knife and sold it."

"Is it possible that Lou Perkins or his dad, Bill Perkins, is behind this?" asked Phoebe.

Everyone looked at her, but no one spoke. "Maybe Bill Perkins killed A.L. Haddon using Earl's knife."

"Why would he do that?" asked Nathan.

"To frame Earl Crenshaw for payback against his father, Robert Crenshaw, for his son dying." said Phoebe.

"Wowwee, that sounds complicated," said Tobias, earning him a hard look from Phoebe.

"Some folks are smart enough to dream up complicated schemes," she retorted.

Nathan tried to choke it off, but a chortle came out of him, earning him a hard look from Tobias.

"All right. Listen up. Tobias, I think the Germans that were fighting lied to you about who paid them. I don't think it was Mad Dog. So, they stole from us. I want you and Nathan to brace them. Do it somewhere with no witnesses. Maybe take them on the way to the saloon or when they're leaving. I'll let you two figure it out. Find out who really paid them to start the fight."

"Yes sir," said Tobias.

"I want to know at the Monday morning meeting."

Tobias and Nathan nodded.

"Phoebe," said Barlow.

"I spoke to Haddon's law partner. He said they don't do criminal work and he couldn't recall any clients who had threatened Haddon."

"Let's move on to the Wardlow case. Tobias, you and Nathan come up with a plan?"

"Yes sir. We sent a telegram to Dependable Investigations asking them to check marriage records at all the ports. Now, we was thinking to send a telegram from Clear Creek to Houston to the hotel where Vano is staying. We was going to say it's from Lavinia and she needs him to meet her in Clear Creek, say at the church."

"That should work, but you need to go up there and make sure the brick plant manager filed a charge against Vano. I'll talk to the district attorney and the sheriff about sending a deputy to arrest him."

"Anything else?"

No one spoke and Barlow said, "Nathan and Tobias. Do what needs doing. Phoebe and I will open the office till noon. If I don't hear from you, I'll see you Monday at breakfast."

Everyone except Phoebe stood and left the office. Phoebe said, "I'm to call Dr. Evans in the morning regarding the pie."

Barlow nodded. "I'll see you in the morning."

CHAPTER 13

"Nathan, what say we meet up after supper and pay a late-night visit out to the Wild Horse saloon. See if our Germans are there?" asked Tobias.

"I'll come to your place, say ten o'clock tonight?" asked Nathan.

"That's fine. Wear your cowboy gear and bring your gun and knife," said Tobias. "We best take our horses."

It was after midnight when the big blonde German, Franz, walked out the back door of the Wild Horse and entered the outhouse. Nathan and Tobias watched from the shadows. When Franz stepped out, Tobias tossed his rope and let it fall over the man's shoulders before he kicked his horse and just like that, the man disappeared into the darkness.

Nathan walked over and picked up the Franz's hat and followed. The German had let out a yell, but no one seemed to have heard or if they did, they paid it no mind.

Walking into the darkness, Nathan found the man, held tight on the ground by the rope around his shoulders; tension being applied by Tobias who talked softly to his horse as though they had a calf on the line.

Nathan walked up to the man, leaned over and placed the barrel of his Peacemaker under the German's nose. "You boys lied. If you want to see daylight you'll speak the truth and you'll be quick about it. Who paid you and your friend to fight?"

The German had been enjoying being drunk, but he was quickly grasping his situation. "The old man. Perkins."

Nathan cocked the pistol.

"He's an old man. Name of Perkins. Man is always complaining about everything and everybody. I ain't seen him lately, but he drinks here."

"If you are lying again, well…."

"No, it was him," gasped the German.

Nathan stood up and said, "We're done." He tossed the German's hat beside him.

Tobias eased the horse back and Nathan pulled the rope free.

Saturday morning, Phoebe and Tobias arrived at the office together. Tobias sat and waited for Barlow and Phoebe picked up the telephone to call the doctor, but the line was in use. She went to her desk and began reading a contract she was working on.

A few minutes later Barlow came in and Tobias followed him into his office.

Phoebe tried the phone again, and the operator said she would ring the doctor's office.

"Hello," said Dr. Evans.

"Good morning," replied Phoebe, her voice unnaturally loud, as though to help it carry over the phone lines. "I was wondering about an appointment. I have felt poorly."

"Why don't you come in today. After work perhaps?"

"Thank you doctor. I think I can slip away this morning if you can see me."

"That will be fine," said Dr. Evans. "Goodbye."

Phoebe's face paled. The pie had been poisoned.

Inside Barlow's office, Tobias related the events of the night before.

"Perkins, was it? It sounds like Phoebe's theory may well be on the money. It would make sense. Perkins is upset that his boy died and blames Crenshaw because he owns the ship. He figures to take Crenshaw's boy away from him because he lost his son. Likely his other son stole the knife from Earl. I just can't figure why kill the lawyer, A.L. Haddon. Why not just kill Earl Crenshaw?" Barlow was silent for a moment. "Well, if there's one thing I've learned, it's you just never know what people are thinking."

Tobias nodded.

"Well done. Monday we will all discuss next steps," said Barlow.

As he stepped out of Barlow's office, Tobias could see Phoebe, still standing at the phone and he knew the pie must have been poisoned. Together they walked to the doctor's office.

"Come in," said Dr. Evans.

"I put your pie out for the cockroaches and mice last night," he said. "I don't know about the mice, but it killed dozens of cockroaches. Full of arsenic."

Back at the office, the two told Barlow what the doctor had discovered.

"It could be one of our clients or opponents. I trust you'll both be watchful," he said, concern on his face. "Why not ask your neighbors if they've seen anyone about?"

"We'll do that," said Tobias, looking at Phoebe.

CHAPTER 14

Saturday, Barlow closed his firm at noon and sent everyone home. "See you Monday," he told them.

Tobias and Phoebe asked Nathan if he and Elvira wanted to come to supper and he accepted. That evening as they ate, Phoebe told them about the poisoned pie. Both were shocked and disturbed.

"Any ideas?" asked Nathan.

Phoebe looked at Tobias, who nodded, and she told them about the woman, Mary Beth. The four discussed it for a while, but Nathan knew her as well and agreed with Tobias; that she and Tobias had attended a couple of dances and had made a trip to the beach, but nothing serious had transpired. She was a nice, well-mannered girl to Nathan's way of thinking.

Barlow ate supper Saturday night in the hotel restaurant with his wife, Sadie. Things had been tense between them since she had pronounced he must give up criminal law work so he could keep regular hours.

"Sam, I've found a house I love. It's three stories and has windows from the floor to the ceiling that open and face the ocean."

"You reckon we need a three-story house?" he asked.

"Sam, we'll need room for some live-in help and the main floor we can use for entertaining." She laughed lightly. "Surely you didn't plan for us to live in a hotel for the rest of our lives?"

"Who are we going to entertain?" asked Barlow.

"Are you just trying to be irritating Samuel? You are a well-known attorney in this town. You are on a first name basis with the city and county leaders. I plan to become more involved with some of the women's organizations. Really Sam, for a man who frequents the theatre and is so well read, you act like you're some sort of, of, uneducated cowboy."

Barlow smiled a terse smile. He took a deep breath and said, "Sadie, I'm thinking, well, that maybe I'm not the fellow you thought I was when you agreed to marry me."

Sadie stared at him, her face reflecting shock. "Oh my, what haven't you told me?"

Shaking his head, he said, "I don't have any secrets. It's just, well, I don't see myself giving up criminal law. Fact is, it's the only part of the law that don't bore me to tears most days. As far as entertaining and that. Well, I enjoy a party as much as the next fellow, but keeping up a big house so we can give parties, well, it don't interest me. Seems like a waste. Live in help? What for? We don't have children; you're a fine cook and I don't mind taking meals out. We can have a lady come in to help with the cleaning. Now I got strong feelings for you, but we need to discuss things, see what we can work out."

Shock registered on Sadie's face. Her mouth opened, but no words came out. She finished her meal in silence, stood and left the restaurant without a word.

Barlow sat thinking. *I've dealt with my share of problems, but I'm adrift this time; drifting out to sea with no idea what to do.*

Finally, Barlow stood, picked up his hat and left the hotel, arriving twenty-minutes later at Robert Crenshaw's house.

Opening the door and seeing Barlow standing there startled Robert Crenshaw, who expected the worse. "Barlow," he said. "What's happened? Has an indictment been issued?"

"Don't be alarmed. I just wanted to ask Earl something. He about?"

"Yes, he's here, Sam. Please, if you hear that Earl's case has come before a grand jury, let me know."

Barlow looked at Robert Crenshaw. He suspected the man would put his son on a ship to Europe if he was indicted, rather than take a chance at trial, but he didn't voice it.

A few minutes later, Barlow was seated at the kitchen table with Earl. "Earl, do you know Lou's daddy, Bill Perkins?"

"Yes sir, I mean to say hello to. I don't hang around their place much. I never did really, but old, I mean Mr. Perkins has been really upset since his oldest boy died. Lou's brother. He was swept off a ship at sea. Mr. Perkins is always cussing everybody and everything these days."

"Did Mr. Perkins or Lou every mention the man that was killed, A.L. Haddon?" asked Barlow.

"No, not that I recall. Weren't he a lawyer? Somebody said that."

"Yes, he was an attorney," replied Barlow.

"Well sir, no offense, but Mr. Perkins seems to hate lawyers. He's always cussing them. Lou said his dad had a farm and a lawyer, working for the bank, took it away from them."

"Did you show Mr. Perkins your knife?"

Earl thought for a minute. "Yes sir, one day I was at their place, on my horse, and just as I was leaving, Lou asked me to show his dad. I dug it out of the saddlebag and showed him. He thought it was right nice."

Barlow thought for a moment and then asked, "Does Lou live with his dad?"

"Yes sir."

"Do you know where Lou works? And his dad?" asked Barlow.

Earl told Barlow.

"Okay Earl, we're making progress, so try not to fret."

Mary Beth had been asked to attend a dance, but she had begged off. Now, on a Saturday night, she told her mother she was going for a walk. She left her house and was now standing across the street from the house Tobias lived in. Lights were on in the house and she could see shadows in the kitchen. Finally, the door opened and see could see Tobias, smiling and laughing. Perfectly healthy. Another couple stepped out on the porch, said their goodbyes and departed. As the door closed, Mary Beth could see that woman from the law office put her arms around Tobias. Anger swelled in Mary Beth.

The next day, Sunday, Tobias asked the neighbors if they had noticed anyone around his house, but no one had.

CHAPTER 15

Everyone from the Barlow firm met for breakfast as usual. No one mentioned it, but everyone knew something was wrong with Barlow. He just wasn't himself. He answered questions and smiled, but he looked like he hadn't slept in days and his eyes didn't smile. Phoebe made a mental note to talk to Elvira, Nathan's wife and Sadie's sister. Something was wrong.

After breakfast, when everyone was seated around the table in Barlow's office, he was about to speak when someone pounded on the law office's door. Tobias opened it to find a small boy holding a telegram. Tobias gave him two-bits and took the telegram into Barlow, who read it silently.

Looking up, Barlow said, "The Earl Crenshaw murder case. Tobias and Crenshaw revisited the Germans, and they changed their story. It seems Bill Perkins paid the Germans to start the fight. At the time the fight broke out, he was in the saloon playing poker with Mad Dog. Now, I think Phoebe had it figured. Either Perkins stabbed Haddon using Earl's knife to frame him or he goaded Mad Dog into it, maybe telling him Haddon was talking about him. Earl says Perkins developed a hatred of lawyers after he lost a farm to the bank."

No one spoke for a minute, then Nathan asked, "If you use that as Earl's defense, I mean, will it work?"

"No, I don't think so," replied Barlow. "Tobias, Nathan, Phoebe. I have an idea. It'll require some acting. Here is what we'll do."

When he was finished, everyone was smiling. "Questions?" asked Barlow. When no one spoke, he continued, "On to the Wardlow saga. This telegram was from Clyde at Dependable Investigations. He hired agents in New York to look into the marriage records there, but they found nothing. However, he asked them to check the immigration records from Ellis Island and they found a Vano Smith and wife, Lavinia Smith. The entered the United States in June 1879."

"Oh my, Vano isn't Lavinia's brother; he's her husband!" exclaimed Phoebe.

"Looks like it," said Barlow. "Which means she committed bigamy and her marriage to DeWayne Wardlow will be invalidated by the state. Providing we can prove it."

"Seems like if DeWayne Wardlow was told, that would bring an end to this situation," said Nathan.

"You'd think so, but he may not be easily convinced. Let's carry out our plan this evening regarding Lou Perkins and his dad, Bill Perkins. That done, we'll see to the Wardlow problem," said Barlow.

That afternoon, after work, Phoebe dressed to the hilt and looking fabulous, was waiting just inside a store, watching for Lou Perkins' approach on his way home. Seeing him across the street and headed her way, she stepped out and crossed the street, turning so that she was walking toward him. Just as she got close, she purposely stumbled, literally falling into his arms and dropping her sun umbrella and the sack of goods she had just purchased. Items rolled out of the sack and over the sidewalk.

Phoebe cried out in pain, and Lou, his face a mask of amazement said, "Miss, miss, what's happened?"

"Can you help me to the bench, I've turned my ankle," said Phoebe.

Lou Perkins carefully assisted Phoebe to the bench in front of the drugstore and turned quickly to gather her spilled items.

"Thank you so much," purred Phoebe, as Lou placed her sack of goods and umbrella on the bench beside her.

"It's no bother," stuttered Lou, almost overwhelmed by the faint odor of Phoebe's perfume and her beauty.

"Would you kindly check my ankle?" she asked, lifting her foot. When she pulled her dress up some eight inches, exposing her leg, Lou felt faint.

Earl Crenshaw had explained to Barlow that Lou Perkins and his dad, Bill Perkins, worked at different places, but arrived home at almost the same time each day. Phoebe's job was to delay Lou for ten minutes while Tobias and Nathan visited his dad at home.

Meanwhile, Bill Perkins had just arrived home when there was a pounding on his door. He opened it to see two men, wearing gun belts, standing there. He noticed the edges of deputy sheriff's badges pinned to their vests; poking out from under their long coats.

He knew that somehow he had been found out. At first fear and then rage consumed him. He stared at the men.

"We're here for Lou Perkins on the matter of the murder of A. L. Haddon," announced Tobias in a hard voice. "Tell him to come on out."

Bill Perkins' face expressed shock and then horror. "Lou? He didn't kill anybody!"

"Says you, old man," growled Nathan. "Witnesses say different. Now get him out here afore we go in for him."

"He had to, ah, he went out to the Wild Horse saloon to visit the girls. He'll be back in a few hours," stammered Bill Perkins.

"Watch him," said Tobias to Nathan, pushing past Perkins and entering the small house. In less than a minute he stepped back out. "He ain't here. Let's go."

With that, Tobias and Nathan mounted their horses, turned them and rode away in a cloud of dust.

Arriving home, Lou Perkins was very surprised to find the house empty. He couldn't figure where his dad had got off to. At that moment, Bill Perkins was at the sheriff's office. He had demanded to see the sheriff and when the deputy told him the sheriff was taking his supper, Perkins had sat down to wait, his face a hard mask.

Twenty minutes later the sheriff walked in and Bill Perkins said, "I want to confess. I stabbed A.L. Haddon. My son, Lou, don't know nothing about it."

The sheriff sat behind his desk, took a bag of tobacco from the drawer, placed a large wad in his mouth and said, "Tell me about it."

"My oldest boy was swept off a ship owned by Robert Crenshaw. If Crenshaw paid more attention to the safety riggings on his ships instead of how much money he makes, my boy would still be alive. So, I decided I'd take his boy. An eye for an eye. I killed Haddon with Earl Crenshaw's knife. I figured he'd be hung or sent to Huntsville for life."

The sheriff spit in a coffee can and asked, "Why kill Haddon?"

"He was a lawyer and I hate lawyers. He hung out at the Wild Horse. Convenient."

The sheriff nodded. "Why not just kill Crenshaw's boy, Earl?"

"That would have been too easy on Crenshaw. I wanted him to suffer like I've suffered. I wanted him to see his boy hung or rot in Huntsville."

"I understand, but why are you confessing?" asked the sheriff. "Seems like your plan was working."

"Don't lie to me. I know you think my boy Lou done it. But Lou didn't know nothing, you hear me! I stole Earl Crenshaw's knife out of his saddlebags. I paid a couple of Germans to start a fight at the Wild Horse and in the medley, I stabbed that low-life lawyer. Now, lock me up and leave my last son be."

CHAPTER 16

Barlow had been in his office less than an hour when a boy arrived with a message from the district attorney, asking him to come by as soon as was reasonably possible. Two hours later, sitting in the district attorney's office, Barlow expressed amazement when the district attorney told him Bill Perkins had confessed to the murder of A.L. Haddon and all charges against Barlow's client, Earl Crenshaw, had been dropped.

"We don't always get it right, Sam," said the district attorney. "I'm just glad we didn't convict an innocent man."

Leaving the courthouse, Barlow met the sheriff, who was entering.

"Say there Barlow, guess you heard about Perkins," said the sheriff, stopping to talk.

"I did," said Barlow.

"Yeah, good news for your client. Funny thing is, after he confessed, old man Perkins got to ranting and raving about my deputies barging into his house. I didn't have a clue what he was going on about, but I don't guess it matters none," said the sheriff, looking intently at Barlow.

"That's odd," said Barlow.

"Yes sir, I find it odd being as how I ain't sent no deputies to Perkins' house."

"Fact is sheriff, I was going to stop by and see you about another matter," said Barlow, changing the subject. "Did the manager of the brick plant, I fear I don't have his name, file a report involving a stolen horse with you?"

The sheriff studied Barlow for a few seconds. "Yes, one of my deputies said the manager, Carlton, is his name, if I remember, came in and said he bought a horse from a fellow and a few days later someone in town claimed it was his horse. Says it had disappeared the day before. Man thought it had gotten out. You representing the horse thief?"

"No sheriff. In fact, I think I know where you can find the alleged thief, if you can spare a deputy tomorrow," said Barlow.

"You know how people feel about horse thieves in this part of the country. I'll be right glad to provide a couple of deputies," replied the sheriff.

"One other thing, sheriff. This alleged horse thief. A woman who claims to be his sister is, as I understand it, his wife. She also recently married a Galveston County boy as part of a scam I'm investigating. She'll be there too."

Startled, the sheriff said, "Damn Barlow. Well, bigamy can get you three years in prison and adultery can bring you a fine of anywhere from one hundred to one thousand dollars. I imagine the district attorney wouldn't mind visiting with this woman. I'll arrest her on your say so. Can you back it up?"

"I can," said Barlow. "I will file a statement with the magistrate this morning, as will one of my assistants who is familiar with the situation."

Back at the office, Barlow called a meeting. After locking the front door, with a note stating the office was closed for the noon meal, Barlow and his team seated themselves at the table in his office.

After staring at everyone around the table, Barlow smiled. "It seems Bill Perkins has confessed to the murder of A.L. Haddon. All charges against our client have been dropped."

Sighs of relief, followed by cheers and laughter filled the room.

"Excellent work by all hands," said Barlow, who looked happy for the first time in weeks.

Barlow let everyone talk among themselves for a few minutes and then called the meeting back to order. "All right, let's see what we can do about making the Wardlow situation right."

"Phoebe, why don't you write the telegram to Vano Smith so it has the woman's touch. Tell him you have to meet tomorrow to discuss an important matter."

"Will do, boss," said Phoebe. "Where and when do you want the meeting to take place?"

"Tobias?" asked Barlow.

"How's tomorrow behind the church in Clear Creek? Let's see. I think a train stops there from Houston on the way to Galveston around ten o'clock. What say ten-thirty?"

"Fine. I'll alert the sheriff. Make sure you send the telegram from Clear Creek so it looks like it's from Lavinia. I'd like for Lavinia and DeWayne to be there and see the arrest. The sheriff may have an arrest warrant for Lavinia. Either way, it would give us a chance to call Vano and Lavinia out regarding their marriage. After you send the telegram, go to Houston and send one to Lavinia from Vano. Tell her he wants her to meet him behind the church at ten-thirty and to bring DeWayne."

Wednesday was clear and cool. Inside the church at Clear Creek, two Galveston County deputies, Tobias, Nathan and Carlton, the brick plant manager, waited. They heard the train whistle and Carlton checked his pocket watch.

"Right on time," said Carlton.

Everyone watched from the church's rear windows and sure enough, Lavinia and DeWayne appeared. They stood talking, appearing nervous. Suddenly Vano Smith appeared, walking fast.

Vano looked around, walked up to the couple and demanded, "What's the problem?"

Total surprise registered on Lavinia's face. DeWayne looked confused.

"That's what I want to know," replied Lavinia.

The two deputies walked out, followed by Tobias, Nathan and Carlton. The deputies had pistols in their hands.

"Don't anybody twitch," said one deputy.

Everybody raise your hands real high and real slow," demanded the other deputy.

"This the fellow sold you a stolen horse?" asked the first deputy, waving his pistol at Vano.

"That's him," said Carlton.

"You are under arrest on suspicion of horse theft," the deputy told Vano, who glared at him.

"You Lavinia Smith?" the other deputy asked Lavinia.

Looking furious, she hissed, "I'm Mrs. DeWayne Wardlow."

"That a fact?" replied the deputy. "Well, Mrs. Wardlow, you're under arrest on suspicion of bigamy."

"Bigamy!" screeched Lavinia.

"Best you say nothing. We'll sort it out down at the office," replied the deputy, handing Tobias a set of handcuffs.

DeWayne looked stricken.

"Do something, DeWayne!" yelled Lavinia.

"Bigamy?" said DeWayne, to no one in particular.

"I reckon Mr. Smith there ain't her brother, but her husband," said Tobias.

DeWayne's mouth popped open and his eyes widened, but he couldn't find his voice.

DeWayne rode to Galveston on the train at Tobias's invitation. Vano Smith sat in one seat, a deputy beside him, Lavinia Smith in another seat, the second deputy beside her. Carlton told the deputies he would come to Galveston to testify when asked. DeWayne sat between Tobias and Nathan who explained their theory: that Lavinia and Van planned to take the money from the sale of his parent's ranch and disappear.

"Are they really married?" DeWayne asked.

Nathan explained seeing Lavinia with Vano in Houston. Tobias told him about the immigration records.

"My folks aren't likely to talk to me again," groaned DeWayne. "What have I done?"

"Ain't nothing unfixable yet," said Tobias. "Talk to your parents. Sign the deed to their ranch back to them. See if Lavinia still loves you after you do that."

That afternoon DeWayne had an emotional meeting with his parents at Barlow's office and signed the deed to the ranch back over to them. When he visited Lavinia in jail and told her, she spit at him and called him a coward and a momma's boy. That evening, DeWayne and his father, carrying a basket of food prepared by DeWayne's mother, walked to the bay to fish.

CHAPTER 17

Their two big cases resolved, Barlow and his team worked hard for two days, clearing up minor investigations and paperwork that had been neglected. Although Phoebe protested the loss of income and business, Barlow declared he was closing the office on Saturday and he expected everyone to enjoy the day off.

Tobias and Phoebe met with Nathan and Elvira and made plans to visit Houston for some shopping and a change to visit a new restaurant or two. Sadie asked Barlow if they could spend the day together and discuss their future plans. He agreed.

Early Saturday morning, while Phoebe was preparing for the train trip to Houston, Tobias went outside to see if he could locate his cats. "Russell!" he called out, looking for the very large orange tabby.

Tobias was walking along the sidewalk when a pretty young lady walked by. He reached up and lifted his hat and as she walked by, he turned his head to watch her for a moment. It was that fact that saved his face, as a shotgun exploded from across the street and he felt pain and a burning sensation as shotgun pellets peppered his arm, chest and neck. He stumbled; a second shotgun blast sounded, the largest group of pellets hitting him lower in the body this time.

Tobias squatted and pulled a revolver from his boot, as he studied the area across the street, looking for the gunman. He saw someone running away, carrying a shotgun. He yelled! When they looked back at the sound of his voice, he saw a face. Mary Beth.

Tobias entered his house and in a calm voice said, "Phoebe, are you there, sweetheart?"

Phoebe walked into the front room to see Tobias sitting in a chair, blood staining his face, shirt and trousers.

"I've been shot," he said, his face pale, "but I'm not hurt."

"Why ain't I dead?" Tobias asked the doctor who was using tweezers to remove lead shotgun pellets from his face, arm, chest and legs, as Tobias groaned and winced, although he was in a bit of a stupor. Using a hypodermic syringe, the doctor had injected him with a large dose of morphine.

"Birdshot," said the doctor. "It's light and small. If it had been bigger shot, you'd likely be a corpse, sure enough. You're lucky. Somehow, you only caught a couple in your face."

"I turned my face. Ah, I was out looking for my cats," explained Tobias, looking at Phoebe in the chair, waiting. *Weren't exactly a lie*, he thought, dreamily. He had been out looking for his cats, although he had turned his head to get a last look at the pretty girl just as the blast hit him. Old habits.

The doctor grunted, focused on his work.

While Tobias was being treated by the doctor, Barlow and Sadie were walking on the beach, talking.

"Sam, I want to apologize and beg your forgiveness," said Sadie.

Barlow looked at her, his face puzzled.

"I do not know what I was thinking, but please let me try to explain. Somehow, it seems I never quite adjusted to my husband, Sweeny's death and the fact that I was a widow. We were only together about a year and I never really faced his death. When you and I met again and my old feelings for you came back, my mind just, well, just somehow it combined my old life with you. Oh, I know you'll think me insane."

Barlow studied her face as they walked, but didn't respond.

Continuing, Sadie said, "Rather than a new life, with a rediscovered love, in my mind I tried to recreate the life I had with Sweeny. He was a successful lawyer also, but he worked for banks. He had a very ordered life. But I've realized you are quite a different man. I would never, ever expect you to change or give up criminal law. You're a man, with a responsibility to support me and a lawyer with a responsibility to your clients. You work as much and when required, please. As to the house…"

Barlow interrupted her.

"I been thinking about the house and I was wondering if maybe I could have a study. A library of sorts. Maybe on the second floor. Does the place have fireplaces? It don't get cold often, but maybe I could have one occasionally."

"Oh Barlow, that would be wonderful. I love the house, but we don't need to entertain," Sadie hurriedly added.

"I've been giving that some thought and I enjoy good conversation and it would likely be a boost for business. Certainly, that would please Phoebe, she can't stand to see me idle. I say let's buy it."

"Thank you Sam. However, I insist we sell some of the railroad stock I inherited from Sweeny to pay for it."

Barlow started to respond, but seeing the set of Sadie's mouth, he just smiled.

Saturday evening, after Tobias had been treated by the doctor and the doctor had taught Phoebe how to administer a morphine injection, the doctor and Phoebe walked outside to find a buggy for hire for the doctor. One came by and the doctor hailed it. Phoebe was pleased to discover the driver was a friend of theirs. He was a young black man, named Isaac who not only drove a Hansom cab for hire, he was the owner. Born a slave, he had been fifteen years old when the Civil War ended. When his parents became sharecroppers, he left, eventually landing in New York where he found work in a livery and later as a Hansom cab driver.

The Hansom's were horse-drawn buggies designed to carry two people, although a third could be squeezed in. The driver sat on a high seat above and behind the passenger cabin. Popular in New York and England, they began to replace the hackney carriages as buggies for hire. Isaac had saved his money, purchased a Hansom and had it transported by ship to Houston so he could rejoin his family. After marrying, he had moved to Galveston. The charge for the one-mile journey from the doctor's office to their home, was fifty cents.

After the doctor had boarded the buggy and said his goodbyes, Phoebe walked out behind her house and close to the outhouses, where she saw a group of boys playing marbles in the dirt. Something they often did when they were at leisure. She paid two of them to go to the train station and find Nathan and Elvira and give them a note.

"You'll know them. They are a very handsome couple about my age and the woman will be wearing a purple hat," said Phoebe, figuring that Elvira would wear her favorite hat for the trip to Houston."

When the boys handed Nathan the note, they said, "It's from a pretty lady."

Nathan handed them each a dime and read the note. Quickly Nathan explained what had happened. He and Elvira left immediately to see Tobias, concern on their faces.

As Elvira and Phoebe talked, Nathan said, "I think I better tell Barlow. He's likely to be angry if we don't let him know."

Phoebe thought for a minute. "I hate to ruin his day, but yes, you're right. Please tell him Tobias is fine."

Both Barlow and Sadie arrived to see Tobias an hour after Nathan found them. They had just returned to their rooms at the hotel Tremont.

Grim faced, Barlow said, "I'll see the city marshal."

"Yes, you go, I'll stay and visit," said Sadie.

Monday morning, everyone, including Tobias was present for breakfast at the Island Café. Tobias's eyes were glazed, as Phoebe had injected him with a small dose of morphine that morning after he insisted on coming to work. Two small, round, anger red wounds were visible on his left jaw.

The one big change that everyone noticed was in Barlow. He was his old self. Happy, assured, enjoying the camaraderie of his team. They had all noticed the affection between Sadie and Barlow over the weekend, while they were visiting Tobias. It seemed the two were constantly touching and looking at each other. Everyone had stayed late Saturday night, keeping Tobias company, visiting and playing dominos at the kitchen table.

After their guests left, Phoebe looked at Tobias and said, "My, a person would think Barlow and Sadie were still on their honeymoon."

Chuckling, Tobias said, "I noticed. I'm surprised they stayed a while rather than hurry back home so they could go to bed."

This time, Phoebe giggled, and exclaimed, "Tobias!"

CHAPTER 18

January turned into February and the Barlow Law Firm kept busy. Tobias healed and Mary Beth was sent up north to an asylum to recover from her mental illness. Barlow and Sadie bought the big, three-story house in the middle of town. You could see the ocean clearly from the upstairs windows and balconies. Workmen spent weeks at the house, building shelves and redoing the kitchen. The Barlows hosted a formal party in their new home the last Saturday in February and it was well attended and considered a huge success.

As March rolled around, a man walked into the Barlow Law office and stood, studying the room. He was in his forties, with black hair slicked back with pomade and a thin mustache. A diamond stick pin flashed in his necktie. He carried a gold-headed cane.

Looking up from a law book she was studying, Phoebe asked, "Can I help you, sir?"

"Hello darling. Name is Yates. Percy Yates. I have an appointment with Barlow."

"Of course. Please have a seat, he should be available shortly," replied Phoebe.

Smiling, Yates walked toward her and stopped only inches from her chair. Leaning over to whisper in her ear, he said, "Sweetheart, I don't know what Barlow is paying you, but I am going to open a business here and I promise you. You can make a lot of money working for me. I'll be in touch."

As he straightened up a smiled, Phoebe replied, "Mr. Yates, the only time I will leave Mr. Barlow's employ is in the event of death. His or mine."

Yates' face showed surprise, then he smiled. "We'll talk," he said, winking at Phoebe, but Phoebe did not return his smile.

A few minutes later, Barlow and a client came out of Barlow's office and walked to the door, talking about the Spring weather. When the man departed, Barlow stepped over to Phoebe's desk and she told him Mr. Yates was waiting.

In his office, with Yates sitting across from him, Barlow asked, "What can I help you with Mr. Yates?"

"Percy. Please. I am a businessman, currently operating three saloons in Houston. I am looking at purchasing some property here, on the island and I need an attorney. To help with the purchase, the legal requirements and other things."

Barlow studied Percy Yates. "Surely you have an attorney," said Barlow.

"I do, but he is disinclined to travel. The man is as large as a bear and finds travel uncomfortable."

"What type business are you planning to start?" asked Barlow.

"Oh, a saloon. I think a man of business should limit himself to what he knows and I know men's weaknesses. Liquor, gambling and women."

"I understand. Will your saloon here in Galveston include all three?"

"Of course. I didn't arrive at your office by chance. I was told that you are on good terms with local law enforcement."

"I appreciate you considering me, but I'll won't be able to represent you," said Barlow.

Very surprised, Yates asked, "Why not?"

"It's a personal thing."

"Oh my. Are you a religious zealot?"

"No, Mr. Yates, I'm not. Just have my own standards."

"So, you think you're all high and mighty! Above the likes of me. Is that it?"

"No, Mr. Yates, we just don't see eye to eye on exploiting other folk's weaknesses, excesses and misfortunes," said Barlow, calmly.

"The hell with you then!" exclaimed Yates, standing, spinning on his heel and striding out of Barlow's door and across the office, his boot heals pounding on the wooden floor. He slammed the door behind him. Phoebe rose and walked into Barlow's office.

"You didn't ask me to complete a client agreement, so am I to assume we will not be representing Mr. Yates?" asked Phoebe, her voice innocent.

"That is correct," said Barlow, looking up at Phoebe. "We disagreed; on principal."

"He can't be all bad; he offered me a job," replied Phoebe.

Barlow laughed.

CHAPTER 19

As Yates was about to step out on the sidewalk at the bottom of the stairs, he had to pause, as two rough-dressed men, who looked like they had just come off the trail, came down the sidewalk. Located just past the stairwell that opened onto the street was the door to the bank, located just below Barlow's second story offices. The two men stepped past the stairwell opening and hesitated in front of the bank, looking in the window. Yates took a second look at them. They didn't appear to be prosperous enough to use a private bank, but then one never knew. There were wealthy farmers and ranchers, not to mention miners, who looked like they didn't have two nickels.

On the sidewalk, Yates walked toward the train depot, fuming over his meeting with Barlow.

Yates had only been gone a few minutes when a man, clearly a farmer or rancher, hesitantly stepped into the office. It was empty except for Phoebe. She watched, and the man seemed about to turn around and leave when she rose and approached him.

"Can I help you sir?" she asked.

"Ah, no. No. I was thinking to talk to the lawyer," replied the man.

"You are in luck, sir. Mr. Barlow is in his office and has a few minutes. Let me just tell him you are here. Your name?"

"Nelson."

A minute later Mr. Nelson was sitting in a chair in front of Barlow's desk, twisting his hat in his hands.

"What can I do for you?" asked Barlow.

Taking a deep breath, the man said, "Well, sir, it's of the most embarrassing nature."

Barlow smiled. "Mr. Nelson, I can assure you I have heard all manner of things and what you tell me is between you and me."

"I was just in the county jail. The judge let me go on my word. I swore in writing that I would be back for my trial if there is one. The judge said I should get a lawyer."

"I handle criminal cases regularly. The cost will depend on what I have to do. How much time is spent and if it is necessary to go to trial."

"I have money. That's not the problem," said Mr. Nelson, looking very glum.

"Very well, what crime have you been accused of?" asked Barlow. "We can go from there."

"First, I want you to understand I didn't do it."

"I understand, Mr. Nelson. Often misunderstandings happen," replied Barlow, to encourage the man to keep talking.

"The charge is, well, I don't know the word for it. The judge said it, but it has to do with me being accused of having relations with an ewe."

Barlow couldn't speak. He needed a minute to process this news. Finally, he said, "You are accused of copulating with a female sheep? Is that what you are saying? Did the judge use the word, 'sodomy'?"

Gloomily, Nelson shook his head up and down.

"Mr. Nelson, don't fret. We'll deal with this. Who was the witness to this alleged event?"

Nelson took a deep breath and said, "My mother-in-law. She went to the sheriff and wrote out a statement against me."

Barlow sat, thinking. Mr. Nelson sat, looking at his hat, sitting in his lap.

"Mr. Nelson, the penalty for the act you've been accused of could range from five to fifteen years in the penitentiary. Do you understand the seriousness?"

Looking up, Nelson, said, "Yes sir. Can you help me? I swear I did nothing except get drunk."

"Mr. Nelson, I will hear you out and then decide if I might be able to help you."

Nelson told Barlow his story. Barlow listened carefully, asked a few questions and said, "My investigators will need to speak to you. Is there somewhere you can meet them tomorrow?"

"I'll be at Simpson's Feed Store about ten."

"That will suit," said Barlow.

A half-hour later, Nelson had signed an agreement, paid a retainer and was on his way home with stern instructions from Barlow to not utter a word about what happened.

"Oh, don't worry," said Nelson. "I ain't eager to even think about it and my wife, she is living in fear that someone will hear about it."

CHAPTER 20

Tobias and Nathan came in from the courthouse where they had been researching land deeds. Barlow called them and Phoebe into his office.

"We have a new client, C. H. Nelson. He's charged with sodomy. Specifically copulating with an ewe."

No one spoke. No one moved.

Tobias leaned over and whispered in Phoebe's ear. "An ewe is a female sheep."

Phoebe's eyes widened.

Barlow continued, explaining, "According to Mr. Nelson, he drank almost an entire bottle of whiskey on Saturday, last. Mainly because his mother-in-law was on the second day of a three-day visit. She berated him for his drinking, so he went out to the barn to escape her. He finished the whiskey and fell asleep. At one point, he undid his trousers to relive himself. He remembers doing that, before he fell asleep again. He awoke from a dream; that he was in bed with his wife and had his hand in her hair." Barlow paused.

Continuing, he said, "Nelson woke up, realized he had ahold of a sheep's wool. He pulled himself up to his knees, but couldn't stand, because he hadn't re-buckled his trousers after he relived himself and they had fallen down around his knees. His mother-in-law had come out to the barn to berate him again. She says she found him on his knees, with his pants down, his hands ahold of the wool of an ewe. She screamed, and he woke up to discover his mother-in-law staring at him, screaming. He admits his pants were down. If he's convicted of sodomy, well, he might be sent to Huntsville for at least five years."

Again, no one spoke.

"We must take this seriously. A trip to Huntsville, well, it would be horrific for Mr. Nelson. Tobias, I want you and Nathan to meet Mr.

Nelson at Simpson's tomorrow at ten. Let him tell the story. Find out about any past behavior that might come to light. See if he visits bawdy houses or the like. Check out the mother-in-law and see if you can visit with the wife. Phoebe, see what you can find on cases involving animals. Any comments?"

No one spoke.

The next morning, Barlow visited the district attorney. "I can't believe you're planning to present this sheep case to a grand jury."

The district attorney looked at Barlow and said, "I sure as hell don't look forward to it. The problem is the witness. Nelson's mother-in-law. She's married to a preacher in Houston and has threatened to inform the Daily News about what she saw. I'm not planning to be the man who showed favor to an alleged sexual deviant who abuses animals. You know people. They will all read every word while complaining loudly it's an unfit subject to be mentioned publicly. No, Barlow. He needs to pled guilty and I'll ask the judge to go lightly on him."

"I'd like a copy of her statement," said Barlow.

Tobias and Nathan met with Nelson.

"You ever visit a bawdy house?" asked Nathan.

"Not since I been married, and that's twenty years," said Nelson.

"Mr. Nelson, I hate to ask, but have you ever, you know, ah, animals?" asked Tobias.

"No, I ain't. I told Mr. Barlow, I was drunk and dreaming."

"Your pants was down. How about your long-johns? Was they unbuttoned?" asked Nathan.

Nelson thought for a minute. "No sir."

Tobias and Nathan took the train to Houston to see Nelson's mother-in-law, whom they found to be reticent. She was firm in her story and told the two men she was saving her daughter from the devil himself. "I am suffering from nightmares about what I witnessed!" she exclaimed.

The district attorney, eager to put the case to rest, was quick to present it to a grand jury. Nelson was indicted and a trial date set. Barlow and Phoebe worked on the case, discussing strategy. They called Nelson in again to discuss the case. When Tobias asked Phoebe about it, she would smile, but wouldn't say anything.

The day of the trial, twelve men sat in the jury box, most of them casting glances at Nelson, as though looking at an insect they had never seen before. The courtroom was full, word having gotten out about the man who had been caught with an ewe. Women held fans in front of their faces as though embarrassed to be present. In fact, several men in attendance, hearing of the charge, had forbidden their wives' attendance. However, a few women friends were present to support Mrs. Oglesbee and a few women were there so they could tell their friends all about it.

"Gentlemen of the jury," began the assistant district attorney, who was trying the case. The district attorney himself had decided not to expose himself to ridicule by trying the case personally. "Sometimes we must bring into the light, something we wish to ignore. But although it may embarrass and pain us to do so, we must. Such a case is before you today. The accused was witnessed abusing a young ewe. When I say abusing, I mean," he lowered his voice, "sexually."

Although everyone in the room knew what Nelson was accused of, a gasp rose from the audience.

The prosecutor called Mrs. Oglesbee, Mr. Nelson's mother-in-law, as his first, and only witness. After establishing who she was and listening to her declare her husband was a minister, to give her credibility, the prosecutor got down to business.

"On the evening in question, you were staying with your daughter and her husband, the accused, is that correct?"

"Yes sir."

"Can you describe the events of the evening?" asked the district attorney.

"Mr. Nelson had been nipping at a whiskey bottle all day. He thought he was being sly, but Isabel, his wife, my daughter, and I saw him several times. By supper time he was very drunk. After we finished our meal, I had reached my limit of patience and called him on his drinking. He said some vulgar things to me and left the house."

"I see. Please inform the court what happened after that."

"Well, my daughter was crying, so I comforted her. Then, after an hour, I decided to have another word with Nelson. I entered the barn. The fence was down so he had penned up a few sheep inside. As I walked in, I looked in a stall. I saw Mr. Nelson on his knees by a young ewe. His trousers were down around his knees and he had a hold of the ewe's wool with one of his hands."

"Did you approach him?" asked the assistant district attorney.

"No, not after I saw them. The animal was to my left and Nelson to my right. I could see everything clearly. I screamed."

"What happened when you screamed?"

"Nelson turned his head and looked at me. He let go the sheep and tried to stand, but his trousers caught and he fell toward me. On his face. I turned and ran back to the house and told my daughter what I had seen."

"Thank you, Mrs. Oglesbee. No further questions."

Mrs. Oglesbee rose, but the judge said, "You must stay there while the accused's attorney questions you."

Mrs. Oglesbee sat.

Barlow approached. "Good morning Mrs. Oglesbee. I just have a few questions to clarify what you saw. First, how far from the defendant and the animal were you when you saw them?"

"Why I was no further than you are from me at this moment," declared Mrs. Oglesbee.

Barlow replied, "Why, that's right close I should think," and he stepped off the distance between himself and Mrs. Oglesbee. "It couldn't be over five or six feet. Are you sure you weren't further away?"

"Absolutely sure. I was almost on top of them," she replied.

"I see, but it must have been very dark in the barn," stated Barlow.

"No sir! We ate early. Sun was still well up. There was plenty of light."

Barlow sighed, "Well then, Mrs. Oglesbee, please describe for the court, Mr. Nelson's male organ at the moment you first saw him and the animal?"

Mrs. Oglesbee's mouth flew open.

A loud gasp came from the audience.

The prosecutor leapt to his feet. "I object your honor!"

Barlow looked at the judge, surprise on his face. "What is he objecting to?" he asked the judge.

"Answer the question, Mrs. Oglesbee," said the judge, his voice matter of fact.

"What am I to say?" she asked, looking at the assistant district attorney.

"I doubt the prosecutor has any idea the answer to my question," said Barlow, and laughter broke out in the audience.

Pounding his gavel, the judge said, "Quiet! Simply answer the question as best you can, Mrs. Oglesbee."

"I don't remember," said Mrs. Oglesbee, her voice showing signs of anger.

"Now Mrs. Oglesbee, you yourself stated you were very close to the defendant, and the barn was well lit. How is it you don't remember? Is it because you never actually saw Mr. Nelson's male organ?"

"I was in shock!" insisted Mrs. Oglesbee.

"I understand, Mrs. Oglesbee. Very well, you said, 'we would understand what Mr. Nelson was doing'. I for one, do not understand. Please explain to me, in detail."

Mrs. Oglesbee turned red, with anger. "You, sir, are a vile man! You will have to answer on Judgement Day!"

"I have no doubt, Mrs. Oglesbee, but in the meantime, please answer the question and might I take this opportunity to remind you. You took an oath in the Lord's name to be truthful about what you saw."

Mrs. Oglesbee clamped her lips shut, squinted her eyes and stared at Barlow, hatred on her face.

"Your Honor, please ask Mrs. Oglesbee to answer the question?"

"I told you what I saw and I'll not say another word!" exclaimed Mrs. Oglesbee.

After Mrs. Oglesbee was allowed to step down, the assistant district attorney informed the judge that the prosecution was complete.

When his turn came for his opening statement, Barlow rose, and slowly walked to the front of the jury box. "Good morning gentlemen. The district attorney's job is to prosecute criminal acts. However, sometimes when the facts reveal themselves, we discover that no crime was committed. That is the case involving Mr. Nelson. Please reserve judgement until all the facts have been brought to light."

"The defense would like to call Mrs. Nelson as our first witness," Barlow announced.

After she was sworn in, Barlow looked at Mrs. Nelson and said, "Mrs. Nelson, have you ever seen your husband show any interest in, ah, animals?"

A reporter from the Daily News was writing furiously.

"You Honor! I object!" yelled the assistant district attorney. "Mr. Barlow is simply trying to embarrass everyone involved."

"Your Honor, this is part of the defense," said Barlow.

"Overruled," said the judge. "Answer the question Mrs. Nelson."

"No, not at all," said Mrs. Nelson.

"I am sorry to be so indelicate Mrs. Nelson, but your husband's situation requires it."

"Please continue," replied Mrs. Nelson.

"I see your hair is curled, Mrs. Nelson. How is that done?"

The assistant district attorney raised his hands in a questioning manner. The judge looked at Barlow.

"Well, I wrap my hair around strips of cloth and tie it at night, to give it the curls."

" I see, it is curly, sort of like a sheep's wool," said Barlow, who appeared to be giving the idea some thought.

The prosecutor had no questions on cross examination.

"Thank you, Mrs. Nelson."

Barlow called as his final witness, the defendant, C. H. Nelson.

All eyes were on Nelson as he walked to the witness chair and swore the oath. After Nelson was seated, Barlow approached him.

"Mr. Nelson, can you tell the jury in your own words what you recall about the evening in question?"

"Yes, sir. My mother-in-law had been at my house for two days and planning to stay for another. On the second day, I took to drinking."

Chuckles and tittering could be heard in the courtroom, coming from the men. The women did not appear amused. The judge ignored the sounds.

"How much did you drink that day?" asked Barlow.

"Might near a whole bottle of whiskey," replied Nelson.

"It has been stated that after supper, you took your bottle and went to the barn. Is that correct?"

"I did. I went to the barn and sat down on the hay in a stall. We got a wooden fence to hold in a few sheep, but it needed fixin, so the sheep was in the barn. I remember finishing the bottle and laying down to sleep."

"What is the next thing you remember, Mr. Nelson?" asked Barlow.

"Ah, at some point, I had to relive myself, and I stood up, but everything was moving, so I just took care of business there in the stall's corner and laid back down."

"Very well, Mr. Nelson. Please continue," said Barlow.

"Well sir, I remember dreaming that my wife and I were in our bed. I had my hands in her hair and then, I heard a scream. I looked around and there in the shadows was an apparition that looked like my mother-in-law. That's all I remember, till I woke up in the middle of the night. Next morning, I went in to breakfast, but there weren't none. I found a note on the table from my wife saying her and her mother was gone to Houston and they would pray for me."

"Thank you, Mr. Nelson, no further questions."

The assistant district attorney, who, by now, knew why the district attorney himself had not handled the case, rose, "I have no questions for the defendant your honor."

"Very well," said the judge.

Barlow stood, walked to the jury box and said, "Gentlemen, it is clear that Mr. Nelson did not commit a crime on the evening in question. I propose to you that under the influence of alcohol, he dreamt. His wife testified she ties her hair up in curls with strips of cloth. During his slumbers, Mr. Nelson reached out and, his hands finding the sheep's wool, thought it his wife's hair."

Barlow hesitated. The room was silent. Everyone listened, fascinated by Barlow's words and his forceful delivery.

Continuing, Barlow said, "In his drunken stupor, during his dream, he rose to his knees. He had no intent to engage the animal and, this is important, he never extracted his manhood from his long johns! The witness could recall nothing about Mr. Nelson's manhood, because she did not see it! There was no crime, gentlemen. Mr. Nelson did not have any desire or intent to engage with an animal and he did not. This is not to cast disparity on the witness. No sir. The witness went out to the barn to give the defendant a piece of her mind and when she saw his trousers loose and his hold on the sheep, she jumped to a conclusion which was not true! A not guilty verdict is the only just decision. Thank you and I apologize to the court and the gallery for the necessity of some of the language."

The assistant district attorney rose to address the jury.

"Gentlemen of the jury, we have an eye witness. Standing only six feet from the defendant in good light. A woman of good reputation who has testified as to the defendant's deviant behavior involving an animal.

Do your duty and find this man guilty so he can try to find redemption during his incarceration."

The jury was herded into a backroom, but returned in less than ten minutes. When the foreman was asked to read the verdict, he stood and declared, "Not guilty."

A minute later, Mrs. Oglesbee, surrounded by her entourage, was wailing and carrying on about the trauma she had endured after witnessing the vulgar event and the mistreatment and embarrassment cast on her by the lawyers and the judge.

Mr. Nelson shook Barlow's hand and turned to see his wife approaching. She slid her arm inside his and the couple walked across the room and out the door.

CHAPTER 21

Barlow and his team had little time to enjoy their victory in court. The next morning, when Barlow arrived, Phoebe was already at her desk and a young, pretty black woman was seated in the outer office.

Barlow greeted Phoebe and nodded at the young woman before entering his office. A moment later, Phoebe entered and closed the door.

"Barlow, the young woman out there waiting is Makena. She's Isaac Brown's wife. The young man who owns the Hansom cab. She needs to talk to you."

Makena Brown was slim and pretty. She sat in a chair across from Barlow and spoke in a soft voice. "Mr. Barlow. Isaac was beaten badly. His face is terrible swollen and he can't speak right, but he whispers a little and he told me to come see you and warn you. He also says you be his lawyer. Maybe help him. We don't know if you help black folks."

Barlow was unprepared for her statement. "Please, continue," he replied.

"He picked up two men and while they were in the cab, he heard one of them say, 'I want this uppity lawyer done away with. Name is Barlow. Got an office close to the courthouse.' Leastwise, that's what I think Isaac is saying."

"Do you know what happened to him?" asked Barlow.

"Some people found him in the street by his cab, all tore up. They thought he was dead. The police came and took him to the doctor. The Negro doctor. I don't know who did it."

"What does the doctor say?"

"Doctor say he don't know. Maybe he live, maybe he die. He all hurt inside."

"Is Isaac at home?"

"Yes sir."

"Where is his horse and buggy?" asked Barlow.

"The police took it to the livery. The one closet to the bay."

"I'm sorry Makena. Certainly, I will do what I can to help. Wait here a moment."

Barlow walked to the outer office and spoke quietly to Phoebe. "When are Tobias and Nathan due back?"

"Anytime," she said.

Barlow repeated to Phoebe what Makena had told him. "Fill out a client form, we are representing Isaac, and when Tobias gets back, have him and Nathan go over to the wagon yard. Pay for the storage of the cab and care for the horse for a couple of weeks. I'm going to see Isaac. Your revolver still there in your drawer?"

"Fully loaded," she said.

"Well, tell Tobias and Nathan about the threat. Ask them to see the doctor. See what he can tell us."

Reentering his office, Barlow asked Makena if he could accompany her home so he could see Isaac and maybe talk to him. She shrugged her shoulders, and they headed out.

Barlow stood over the bed, looking down at Isaac. The young man was so badly beaten, Barlow didn't recognize him. His eyes were swollen shut. The doctor had stitched gashes above his eyes. His face was swollen to the size of a melon. Barlow sat in a chair beside the bed.

"Isaac, it's Barlow. If you can hear me, just squeeze my hand." Barlow reached over and took hold of Isaac's hand. He felt Isaac squeeze it.

"Good. Now rest easy. I've talked to Makena, and she told me what you overheard and I'll be watchful. Thank you. We've seen to your horse and cab and I will talk to Makena and find out what she needs until you get better."

Isaac squeezed Barlow's hand. Then Barlow saw his lips moving. He leaned his ear down to Isaac's mouth. Isaac whispered. Barlow frowned.

"Isaac, did you say the man had a thin mustache?" Barlow felt pressure on his hand. I understand. Did he have his hair combed back with pomade?" Again, pressure on his hand. Was he carrying a gold-headed cane?" A squeeze.

"Thank you Isaac. I know who he is. Is he the man that did this to you?" A squeeze.

"All righty. Now you rest for a bit."

Isaac's lips moved and once again, Barlow put his ear close to Isaac's mouth.

"Other man was big with strange ears?" asked Barlow.

Isaac squeezed his hand.

Later, at the office, Barlow discussed the situation with Phoebe, Tobias and Nathan. "A man I declined to represent, Percy Yates, might well be planning to have me killed. It also appears that he and perhaps a man accompanying him beat Isaac badly. Tobias were you and Nathan able to see the doctor that treated him?"

"Yes sir. The doctor said Isaac appears to have been kicked and stomped. He figures if nothing is ruptured inside, he might live, but it don't look like it to the doctor. Says his body is black and blue from bleeding inside."

Barlow described Yates to everyone and told them that Yates claimed to own three saloons in Houston. "I'm guessing in the Happy Hollow area of town," said Barlow. "Tobias, you and Nathan head up there and see what you can find out, but be right careful asking questions about Yates. If you can locate him, see if there is a big fellow with 'strange ears' about. Don't wear them fancy new suits. Dress as cowboys, looking for a good time. Spend the night. Phoebe, give them some extra expense money from the cash box to spend on drinks and a little faro."

Phoebe eyed Nathan and Tobias. "I'll be needing an accounting of the money and I want to remind you boys you're married men."

Nathan and Tobias nodded. Both feared Phoebe.

When everyone had returned to their work, Barlow walked into his private office and removed the Welby Bulldog from its shoulder holster under his jacket. He carefully checked it, although he had done so several times over the weeks. The pocket pistol sported a five-inch barrel and carried five rounds. The double-action revolver was reported to be accurate up to forty-five or fifty feet and Barlow had shot the weapon several times and found this to be true, but he figured if he needed it, chances were, it would be at a much closer range. After giving it some thought, he didn't understand what Percy Yates would gain by having him killed, but murders had been committed over less. It was likely that someone would try to shoot him with a rifle from a distance or catch him alone and unawares and shoot him up close so they would be sure to kill him.

Barlow sighed. *The world was a wonderful, but often scary place*, he thought.

Phoebe stepped into the office. "Barlow, I thought to step out for a bite. Can you manage for a bit?"

Surprised, because she rarely left the office, Barlow replied, "Of course. Take your time."

CHAPTER 22

Married life had become everything Barlow had dreamed of. A partner to share experiences and meals with. Someone to talk to about mundane things and subjects and activities they both enjoyed. He had been a bit put off at the changing of his routines, but he had settled into new ones. He debated telling Sadie about the potential threat and decided he must, for her own safety. Over supper in their home, prepared by a new live-in cook and housekeeper, Barlow explained about Percy Yates and Isaac.

Sadie took the news calmly. "I trust you have a plan to deal with this? I don't suppose the district attorney will act on the word of a Negro."

Barlow smiled. "No, the district attorney would be appalled if I asked him. I'm working on the situation. Fact is, if it becomes clear that Yates intends on doing me harm, I do have an idea or two."

Sadie looked up from her food. "Sam, take care. Please."

Tobias and Nathan, from all appearances, were two down on their luck cowboys, as they stepped off the train in Houston and made their way to Happy Hollow, the area of Houston that was home to saloons, gambling dens and bawdy houses.

"You got a pencil?" Tobias asked Nathan.

"In my pocket," replied Nathan.

"We'd best keep good track of our spending," said Tobias.

"I hear ya. I sure don't want to git crossways with Phoebe."

"I don't either," said Tobias. "Two things that get that woman riled is somebody not working hard and somebody wasting money."

The two took a room and then split up to cover more saloons. Nathan drank a beer at three different saloons, asked a few questions at each, complimenting the place, casually asking who owned it and kept his eyes open, but didn't have any luck. One saloon was owned by the bartender himself, another by a businessman named Ashworth. "Bit of a hard case," said the barkeep, and Nathan chuckled. At the third, a well-dressed man held court at a corner table. Two men and two women sat with him, laughing and drinking.

Leaning in a little, Nathan said to the bartender, "Little party going on there sounds like."

Nodding, the bartender replied, "Most nights. That's Henderson. Made his money in land speculation. Owns the joint."

Tobias bought drinks for two dance hall girls, paying for whiskey although he knew they were being served tea. He followed the same process as Nathan, only he asked the girls if they knew who owned the saloon they were in.

"Hell, if I know, some old man. And I mean old; handsome," said the girl sitting at Tobias's table, rubbing her hand over Tobias's face.

"Old huh," replied Tobias.

"Walks with an old curved stick and has a man help him walk. He comes in most nights to see how busy we are and count the money."

Tobias smiled, and said, "Sweetheart, as much as I regret it, I gotta go."

At the second saloon, Tobias was talking to a dance hall girl and had just ordered her a second 'whiskey' when a large, but solidly built man appeared at the bar and ordered a sarsaparilla. It wasn't the fact that the man didn't order alcohol that caught Tobias' attention. It was the man's ear. It looked deformed. When the man turned, leaned on the bar and sipped his drink, Tobias could see his other ear also looked mutilated.

Tobias had seen men whose ears were disfigured. In Asia, the unarmed combat devotees often suffered from damaged ears because of the multitude of blows they suffered in training and contests. However, this man likely fell into the second group that Tobias had observed. Professional fist fighters. There was money to be made if you could win at boxing, but it often took a toll and sometimes claimed fighter's lives.

Tobias made light conversation with the girl while keeping an eye on the big man. In a few minutes a man who could only be Yates joined him at the bar. Carrying a gold-headed cane, the man was dressed like a dandy, sported a thin mustache and his dark hair was combed straight back.

"Who is the fancy dressed fellow at the bar?" Tobias asked the girl.

She turned, looked and said, "Oh, that's Percy. He owns the place. The big man is Bruno. He works for Percy. They aren't nice men. They hurt the girls."

CHAPTER 23

Tobias and Nathan spent the night in Houston, but both were happy to leave the next morning to return to Galveston. They made it back to the office after the noon meal, still dressed as cowboys right off the trail. Barlow was with a client and Phoebe gave Tobias a smile, but focused on her work.

Once they were shown into Barlow's office, Tobias told him what they had discovered. Barlow listened and said, "Well, I can't sit around worrying. I'll keep an eye out. Why don't you two see if Isaac is holding on?"

After Tobias and Nathan left, Phoebe brought a young woman in to see Barlow and introduced her as Mrs. Fredricks. "Have a seat Mrs. Fredricks. I'm Sam Barlow, how can I be of service?"

The girl was young, dressed in a clean, but inexpensive dress. "I don't know if you can help me, but my aunt said I should see a lawyer to find out."

Barlow nodded and waited.

"My husband, Terrance, well, let me start over. My momma died years ago and my daddy raised me. He died last month and left me his life savings, almost three thousand dollars. I've been married to Terrance for two years and we have a little boy, Terrence Junior. Terrance, well, he don't work steady. He drinks. I loved my daddy, but the money was such a blessing. Sometimes there ain't enough to eat or we have to move cause the rent's past due. I put the money in the bank, but Terrance took it out. All of it and now, he's disappeared. I guess he'll come back when he's drank up all the money. Please understand, Mr. Barlow. Terrance is good to us and loves us, it's just the drink. He can't help himself."

Barlow sighed. "Mrs. Fredricks, under the law, any money you inherit is your personal property, however your husband, being the man, may manage it any way he sees fit. That said, I don't think the law will help you get your money back. However, if he is not providing for you and the child, we can file against him in county court and get a court order, requiring him to provide, since your property has value."

She began to cry. "My son and I. What will become of us? We don't know where Terrance is and he won't care about a court order. If you find him, he might pay a month's rent and buy some food, but then he'll disappear again with whatever money he ain't drank up."

Barlow had dealt with drunkards, deadbeats and worthless men on many, many occasions. He knew the law would be of no help in Mrs. Fredricks case. "How long ago did your husband take the money from the bank and disappear?" asked Barlow.

"Two days ago," said Mrs. Fredricks, holding a handkerchief to her face. "The rent is due in a week, and we have enough food for another week, but I don't know what we'll do after that. My aunt has helped some, but she is a widow and don't have much."

Barlow thought for a moment and decided. "Mrs. Fredricks, let me have my clerk look into the law and see if there is something else that can be done."

"Thank you, sir, but I can't pay you unless I get some money back."

"As I said, your husband has the legal authority to manage your in-herited property, but give me a few days and let me look into the situation. You'll owe nothing if we are unsuccessful, but if we are, would you be amendable to paying the firm for our expenses and ten percent of the recovered money?"

"Oh my, yes, Mr. Barlow."

"Please describe Mr. Fredricks and do you know where he likes to drink? We might need to serve him with legal papers."

Tobias and Nathan found Isaac alive and improved. His wife, Makena welcomed them when they told her they worked for Barlow. "He was asking me to see if Mr. Barlow would come talk to him, but he can talk to you, can he not?"

"I reckon. Leastwise, we can start and see what it's to do with," said Tobias.

"Hello Isaac, we work for Mr. Barlow. He sent us over here to check on you."

Isaac tried to smile, but his face and lips were still badly swollen. "Need to tell Mr. Barlow about them men," he said, his voice hoarse.

"It's okay, you likely don't remember, but you done told about the threat on his life," said Tobias.

"No, I mean, yes, I remember, but the man was furious and said he wanted it done soon. He told the big man, 'Make sure he knows it was Percy Yates that ordered his death afore he dies'. I been saying the name over in my mind so I don't forget it."

Tobias and Nathan looked at each other. "How d'you come to fight with them?" asked Nathan.

"Oh, I took them where they wanted to go in my cab and stepped down and opened the door. They got out, and I told them the fare was one dollar. The man with the cane said, 'I ain't paying no Negro a dollar' and threw two-bits on the ground. Then they walked away. I reached out and grabbed his arm. He turned and hit me in the head with his cane. Afore I knew it, I was on the ground and the two of them was stomping and kicking me."

Tobias reported back to Barlow, who accepted the news with a smile. "Excellent," he said. "I'd much rather put this threat to bed now than have to keep thinking about it. No to mention how good it is to hear Isaac is recovering. Tobias, if this ex-fighter, Bruno, tries to kill me, I doubt he'll be the type to turn on his boss, so I want to have something ready. Most times, threats are just idle talk, but just in case, I'd like you to make some inquires. But it is my intentions to deal with Mr. Yates even if he doesn't try to kill me, because of what he did to Isaac Brown."

Tobias and Nathan started at Barlow.

"On a more pressing issue, I need you two to locate a drunkard and relive him of every penny he has. If we find him soon, he should have something just less than three thousand dollars on him. Now, we need to develop a plan. It wouldn't do for you two to be seen with him. Once he discovers his money is gone, he'll take to hollering about being robbed. It appears he usually drinks down at the Seaside Saloon when he's flush. I would guess he'll have a room next door, at the Seaside Inn. I expect that's where you'll find him. Age is twenty-five. Name is Terrance Fredricks. Thin, long hair, but not much of a beard. Wears a bowler hat."

Phoebe stuck her head in the office door. "I'm leaving Barlow, unless you need something."

"No, I'll see you tomorrow," said Barlow, smiling, but thinking, *what has gotten into Phoebe?*

CHAPTER 24

Tobias dressed as a sailor on shore leave, while Nathan dressed in his new suit. The two waited until almost ten that night, to leave their homes. They traveled separately. Both walking to avoid any record of their activities. Tobias entered the Seaside Saloon, ordered a beer at the bar and sipped it while studying the room. Terrence Fredricks was easy to spot. He was at a table in the corner, two bottles of whiskey sitting on it, one empty, the other almost full. Two men sat with Terrence while he waved his hands and talked. It appeared he was explaining something to his two drinking companions.

Nathan waited across the street. When Tobias did not appear after twenty-minutes, it was a sign that indeed, Mr. Fredricks was inside, indulging in drink. After putting his pocket watch back in place, Nathan walked next door to the Seaside Inn and entered. It was late, and the clerk was asleep in a room behind the counter. Nathan had planned to distract the man and look at the guest register, or bribe the man, but he saw it wasn't necessary. Walking quietly behind the counter, he picked up the register and a pen and signed, 'W. A. Bartholomew'. After looking at room numbers, he saw Fredricks was in number 4 on the first floor. Number 8 was open on the second floor, so he put room 8 by his name and took the key from the wall behind the counter. He placed three dollars in the register, closed it and replaced it under the counter.

Quickly, he grabbed the key to number 4 and in less than a minute he was in Fredricks's room. A minute later he had discovered the hidden money and placed it in his pockets. He left, went upstairs, entered room 8, ruffled the bed and dropped the key on it. Downstairs, the clerk was still asleep. Nathan smiled. *Sometimes, things go your way*, he thought.

Nathan was waiting in the shadows, out of the way of the gaslights, when Tobias walked out and standing to one side, built a quirly. When his match flared, Nathan could see his face. A moment later, three men, holding each other up, stumbled out of the saloon. Nathan lit a match and held it for a second, to let Tobias know for sure it was done. Seeing Tobias walk away, Nathan began walking himself. The two men walked to their respective homes.

The next morning, Tobias and Nathan sat in Barlow's office, smiling.

"I judge by your expressions and the fact that you are not in jail, that you were successful," said Barlow.

"Yes, sir," said Tobias.

Nathan stood and placed a small stack of money on Barlow's desk. "Exactly two-thousand, seven hundred dollars," he said, before sitting back down.

"Gentlemen, this money is the property of our client, Mrs. Fredricks. We are simply assisting in its return to her," explained Barlow. "It seems her husband, by some error in judgement, took it with him rather than leave it safely in the bank."

"God's work," said Tobias.

Later that morning, after Phoebe had calculated the expenses involved, which amounted to three beers at the saloon for Tobias, and three dollars for the room, she determined the balance to be two thousand, six hundred and ninety-four dollars. The firm's ten percent came to two hundred and sixty-nine dollars and forty cents.

A boy was sent to fetch Mrs. Fredricks, who arrived quickly, with her child, Terrence Junior.

"Mrs. Fredricks, mysteriously, I have come into a certain amount of money. I am giving it to you as a gift to do with as you see fit, but my counsel is that perhaps you should be cautious."

Mrs. Fredricks looked at Barlow, disbelief, then understanding on her face. "Have you ever died, Mr. Barlow?" she asked.

"Died and was brought back, you mean? Why, I'm not sure," replied Barlow, surprised by the question. "To be frank, I have been seriously injured more than once, to the point I lost consciousness."

"I believe in angels, sir. I think some folk are born angels, but some die and return as angels. I believe with all my heart you are an angel. It might be the others in your office are angels as well."

Barlow smiled. "Thank you for the kind words, but there are a good many people would disagree with you on me being an angel."

She smiled and after a moment, said, "Sir, I thank you for the gift. I am a married women and cannot accept such a large gift, all at once. Is there a way I could receive it in small increments each month?"

"After a visit to the privately owned bank housed below Barlow's law offices, accompanied by Phoebe, Mrs. Fredricks left with an account in her baby son's name, Terrence Fredricks Junior, listing her as the custodian of the account until his majority. The sum of two thousand, four hundred and twenty-four dollars and sixty-cents was in the account.

Terrence Fredricks the senior, arrived home at noon the following day, sick from lack of alcohol, and in great distress as he confessed to his wife that he had taken all the money from the bank and it had been stolen.

Stone faced, she told him, "You'd best find work. We've food enough for five or six days and the rent will be due. I have a bit of whiskey to steady you, Terrence, but work you must have, today."

Knowing he would be home today, she had poured some whiskey from one of the bottles she had hidden from him, time to time, when he was passed out, into a glass. She found it and he drank it eagerly.

"I talked to Henry at the general store this morning. He mentioned he had two wagons of goods arriving this afternoon. Might be he'll let you unload them. Bring home the money. I might find a little whiskey for you. If you don't, well, Terrence, don't come home. We won't be here. We'll move in with my aunt."

Terrence nodded, put on his hat and left. *He's sick. I must take charge and see to him as well as myself and Junior*, thought Mrs. Fredricks.

CHAPTER 25

Barlow had made light of the threat against his life, but he took it seriously. He studied the area from an upstairs window before leaving his home in the mornings and stood in the stairwell leading up to his office, surveying the area before stepping out onto the walkway. He had hired the Pinkerton agency to place men at the rail depot in Galveston, watching for arriving persons fitting the description of Bruno, the man with the deformed ears. He figured it was worth the cost to keep a watch for two weeks, just in case Percy Yates' threat was real.

A week later, a boy appeared in the office and handed Phoebe a note. She read it, tipped the boy two-bits and walked into Barlow's office. She held out the note. "This just arrived," she said.

Barlow read it and smiled. "Excellent," he said. "When Tobias and Nathan return from the courthouse, I'd like to see them."

Two hours later, Tobias and Nathan were in Barlow's office.

"The Pinkerton's said a man matching Bruno's description arrived on the morning train. The man on duty followed him. He took a cab to a hotel close to our office. The Empress. After an hour, he exited and went for a walk, which took him past our place of business. He is now having his noon meal."

"You thinking he's here to kill you?" asked Tobias.

"Yes, I think so, and he's likely to do it when I'm coming in or leaving. He might plan to follow me and see if an opportunity shows itself. Let's make sure he has his chance. I'm thinking he will linger nearby at the end of the day, follow me to see what my routine is. He does not know that I know who he is or that he is planning to kill me. He will be confident and brazen. I think I will leave at six today and walk to the Tremont hotel and stay the night there. Nathan, please go to my home and explain to Sadie. Ask her to send a clean shirt and my kit to the hotel. I may be there a few days. I would like you boys to trail me from work to the hotel and back here in the mornings. I'll leave the hotel at six in the morning and walk here. One of you in front and one behind in a cab would likely be best. If he makes an attempt, I would rather like to capture him, but of course if necessary we'll do as we must." Barlow thought for a moment. "No, the sun rises before seven in the morning and sets before seven in the evening. I'll leave the hotel at five-thirty. I want to make sure it's dark to encourage Bruno to make his move."

Barlow, Tobias and Nathan carried out their plan that evening. Nathan was a block ahead and Tobias a block behind Barlow when he left work and walked leisurely to the hotel. He checked in, received his kit from the concierge, settled in his room and was having supper in the hotel dining room, when Tobias walked in and sat down.

"Howdy boss," he said. "Bruno followed you to the hotel, waited a bit and then returned to his own hotel. Nathan will be there in the morning, waiting and I'll be outside, waiting for you to come out."

Barlow smiled. "Would you like some supper?"

"No thank you, I'd better be getting on home," said Tobias.

The following morning, Barlow ate breakfast at five and at five-thirty exited the hotel. He didn't see Tobias, but calmly walked to his office. Later that morning, Tobias and Nathan appeared and when Barlow had a free minute, they reported the morning's activities.

"He left his hotel at five and took a cab to the Tremont," said Nathan.

"I saw him arrive," said Tobias. He was in the lobby, hiding behind a newspaper when you left this morning. He followed you on foot all the way to the office. Do you know the abandoned warehouse?"

"Sure," said Barlow. "That is surely a deserted area, especially that time of morning."

"He stopped for a minute there, looked around. I'm thinking he might be waiting there."

"Let's do the same thing tomorrow. Nathan, if he goes straight to the warehouse, set up across the street, but don't spook him. I want to be done with this."

CHAPTER 26

Everything unfolded much as they had imagined it. Bruno stepped out of the cab, six or seven blocks from the warehouse. Nathan, following in another cab, passed Bruno, debarking a block past the warehouse. He quickly walked back and, as Barlow instructed, hid across the street, armed with a hefty club and his revolver. He watched Bruno arrive and look around for a hiding place. He settled on a doorway.

Barlow walked slowly as he approached the warehouse, the surrounding area, unlit by streetlamps, was very dark. Tobias moved up beside Barlow, but Barlow was close to the street and Tobias was almost touching the building, six feet separating the two men. Barlow saw the deep shadow of the doorway. The only real danger was of Bruno stepping out and shooting him. Barlow had his Welby Bulldog in his hand, cocked, ready to fire. Tobias, on Barlow's left, had a wooden club in his left hand and his revolver in his right, as he moved ahead of Barlow. Three feet from the dark doorway, he slammed the club into the side of the building, creating a very loud noise.

Barlow stopped. Tobias shoved his revolver into his waist band and quickly stepped forward, both hands holding the bat in the manner of baseball players, high and to his right. Startled by the loud bang, Bruno took two quick steps out of the doorway onto the wooden sidewalk. Moonlight glinted on a gun barrel. Bruno pointed his revolver, waving it, looking for his target in the dark, but just as he fired, Tobias swung in and down, fast and hard, hitting Bruno's arm. Bruno screamed in pain; the gun's loud report breaking the early morning quiet. Barlow stepped forward holding his own gun. Nathan appeared; his revolver pointed at Bruno.

Tobias swung the club up and hit Bruno in the head. Bruno stepped back, unsteady on his feet. A knife appeared in his hand. Tobias stepped back, dropped the club and drew his gun. Bruno saw three dark shapes around him, all holding revolvers, pointed at him. A few minutes later, Bruno was sitting against the wall of the building, well trussed, his hands tied behind him, his legs tied together and a kerchief in his mouth, because he wouldn't stop cursing and yelling threats.

Tobias and Nathan built smokes as they studied Bruno. "Boss, I don't understand why we took such a chance. Why didn't we just shoot the fool?" asked Nathan.

"Well, Nathan, it was a risk, for sure, but I need to know for sure that Percy Yates is behind this," replied Barlow.

After a while as it was getting dark, Barlow walked over to Bruno, removed the kerchief from his mouth and said, "Bruno, I know the judge and the district attorney. Intent to murder and conspiracy charges are going to put you in Huntsville prison for a long time. I've heard it's not a pleasant place."

"I didn't do anything!" yelled Bruno. "I thought you was fixing to rob me!"

"That right? Is that why you followed me yesterday and today?" asked Barlow. "Pinkerton agents and my men have been on you since you got off the train. I can produce a strong case against you. Your only hope is to tell me, right now, who sent you to kill me. Given your cooperation, I'm going to be inclined to ask the district attorney to allow you to plead guilty and to ask for a minimum sentence."

"Go to hell!" yelled Bruno.

"Or, we shoot you right now," replied Barlow, his voice matter of fact.

"You're a lawyer!" said Bruno. "You can't just shoot a man."

"Oh, I'm not going to shoot you, Bruno. He is," said Barlow pointing at Tobias, who grinned and pulled his gun from his holster.

"Justified shooting. He shot you to save my life," said Barlow.

Tobias raised his gun and Bruno said, "Hold on, damnit! Yates. Fellow name of Percy Yates. I don't know what you done to him, but he wants you dead. I work for him, but he promised me an extra hundred dollars to kill you."

Barlow smiled. Tobias looked disappointed. Nathan took a drag on his quirly.

"We know Yates owns some saloons in Houston. Which one does he usually do his drinking in?" asked Barlow.

"The Stallion," replied Bruno.

Two hours later, Bruno was in the county jail and Barlow was talking to the district attorney, telling him what had transpired.

"Risky, Barlow. He might have hit you with his shot," said the district attorney.

"Yes, but we had the situation in hand," replied Barlow.

"If I can get Bruno to testify against this Yates fellow, I have a chance at him," said the district attorney. "I'm going to add conspiracy charges."

"It'll be his word against Yates, but I sure hope you get it done," said Barlow. "I told Bruno I'd ask you to go easy in exchange for his guilty plea and cooperation."

"I can do that," agreed the district attorney. "Fact is, I could indict them for the assault on Isaac Brown, but you know that wouldn't get far with a jury. A black accusing white men of attacking him for no reason. I would lose face, just bringing the charge. So, Bruno pleads guilty, but if he gets stubborn, I'll have no problem convicting him with the testimony of you and your men. I'll let you know about Yates. I have a grand jury in session. I'll talk to Bruno tomorrow and run it by the grand jury the next day. Won't be a problem to get an indictment. As soon as I do, I'll issue an arrest warrant and have the Harris County deputies pick him up."

"Appreciate it," said Barlow. "Reckon I better be getting on to work."

At the office, Barlow met with Tobias and Nathan. "Fine work, gentlemen. Tobias, I don't want to chance Yates disappearing. I wouldn't know who he was sending for me next and I'm not likely to be so lucky if he gets another chance at me. I reckon we need to go with the plan and it'll have to be tomorrow. When he doesn't hear from Bruno, Yates will make inquiries. I don't want him to disappear. Can you and Nathan manage it?" asked Barlow.

"For sure," said Tobias. "Tomorrow night."

CHAPTER 27

The next afternoon, Tobias and Nathan were unrecognizable. Dressed in run-down boots, filthy hats and greasy trousers, the two sat by themselves at the back of a train car on the way to Houston; other passengers looking at them with distaste. In Houston, the two claimed their baggage, a large, battered trunk with two locking leather straps. They hired a buggy to take them to Happy Hollow where they rented a room at a run-down hotel. In the room, they discarded the stones that they had placed in the trunk in Galveston.

A block away, they entered the Stallion Saloon and took a table, but they didn't see Yates. They sipped beers for an hour before he appeared and sat at a table. The bartender brought him a gill glass and a bottle of whiskey without being summoned. As the night progressed, several men and women who worked in the Stallion, stopped by Yates' table, sometimes staying for a drink.

Finally, as it neared midnight, Tobias ordered a glass of good whiskey. When he saw Yates fill his own whiskey glass, Tobias picked up his glass of whiskey, rose and announced, "I'm going out back to take care of business," in a slurred voice.

"Why, I reckon I'll join you," announced Nathan, picking up his glass of beer. As the two stumbled toward the back, they came even with Yates' table. Nathan bumped into Tobias, dropped his glass of beer on the floor and yelled, "Hellfire! Watch yourself!"

Tobias fell across Yates' table, knocking the mostly empty bottle of whiskey onto the floor. Yates automatically half-stood to avoid Tobias. "You damn heathen!" yelled Yates. "Get the hell off my table!"

Tobias straightened up, mumbled an apology and staggered away. Yates picked up his glass of whiskey and drank it in two large swallows.

The bartender appeared with a fresh bottle and refilled Yates' glass. Yates threw this one back in one gulp and said to no one, "I'm going home."

When Yates came out of the saloon, carrying his gold-headed cane, Tobias and Nathan were waiting in the shadows. A block away, Yates stumbled, and they were there to wrap his arms around their shoulders. At their hotel, they helped Yates to their room. By this time, he was completely asleep.

"I reckon you made the switch," said Nathan, admiration in his voice. "What did you say was in the drink you gave him?"

"Chloral hydrate. A sedative. He should be out a good eight hours, what with the whiskey and the large dose I put in the drink," said Tobias.

After reliving Yates of a derringer, they found in his pocket, and a knife strapped to his arm, they placed Yates in the trunk, along with his cane, closed it and secured it with the leather bands.

Early the next morning, Tobias put a smaller dose of chloral hydrate in a glass, added a shot of whiskey and held it to the man's lips until he opened his mouth. Tobias slowly poured it in Yates' mouth until he swallowed. They loaded the trunk onto a buggy and asked to be taken to the train station. When they arrived in Galveston, they hired a cab to take them and their trunk to a hotel downtown, close to the courthouse. Boys who worked for the hotel carried the trunk up to the room. The hotel was rather low-rent, so no one questioned their rather shabby dress. In the room, they removed Yates from the trunk and put him on the floor. He was completely out, but breathing steadily. They trussed him with rope, tied a gag across his mouth and placed a feed sack over his head. They left and reported to Barlow.

"All done, boss, no problems. He had these in his pocket," said Tobias, laying the derringer and dagger on Barlow's desk.

Barlow picked up the double-barreled derringer and studied it. It was a Remington Model 95, over and under that fired a .41 short cartridge. "I've a thought," said Barlow. "Put the knife back if you will."

"Sure boss," said Nathan.

"He'll think we failed to discover it. Tobias, you boys will need to keep an eye on Yates. Some water if he can swallow. I'm going over to the courthouse now to see the district attorney. Hopefully, he'll get the indictment on Yates this morning and have the arrest warrant by this afternoon."

CHAPTER 28

Bruno talked and talked, blaming everything on Percy Yates. The district attorney took him before the grand jury the following day. The grand jury indicted Bruno on assault with intent to murder and conspiracy charges for conspiring with Yates regarding the murder of Barlow. The jury also indicted Yates as an accomplice to the assault with intent to murder and for conspiracy. At two o'clock, the district attorney came out of the jury room to find Barlow in the hallway.

"I guess you're anxious Barlow. Not to worry. I have indictments on both men and I'll have an arrest warrant for Yates within the hour."

"That's good news. The reason I'm here is I was told that Yates was seen right here in Galveston."

The district attorney stared at Barlow, suspicion on his face. "I see. Could be he's looking for Bruno. Where was he seen?"

"He was in a hired buggy, somewhere around Market Street I think," said Barlow.

"Barlow, I'm not even going to ask who told you. I'll just assume it's likely true," said the district attorney. "After I get the warrant signed, I'll notify the city marshal."

"Just trying to support law and order," said Barlow, smiling.

Returning to his office, he sent one of the young boys who were always about with a note to the hotel where Tobias and Nathan were sitting with a still unconscious Yates. Upon receiving Barlow's note, Tobias and Nathan untied Yates, replaced his knife and helped him downstairs and out to the street. He was mumbling. Nathan hailed a cab, and they put Yates in it, putting his gold-headed cane beside him.

"We don't know him, was just drinking with him is all. Here is five dollars. Can you just drive him around town till he comes to and says where he wants to go?"

"Sure," said the driver, paying little attention, but glad to get a five-dollar fare. If the man didn't come to after a while, he would simply put him out on the sidewalk.

Yates came to less than an hour later. His head hurt immensely, he felt sick and was terribly confused and disorientated. "Where are we going?" he asked the driver.

"Where would you like to go, sir?"

Yates looked around. "Where are we?"

"Downtown Galveston sir. Would you like to ride along the sea? It's a nice day."

Yates tried to think, but his head hurt so bad, it was difficult. *He remembered drinking at his saloon in Houston, the Stallion. Where the hell was Bruno? Oh, he remembered. Bruno was in Galveston to kill that low-life lawyer, Barlow. But why was he, Yates in Galveston? He had gotten drunk before and awoken with no memory of the night before, but he had never traveled this far. I probably got to thinking to come down here to see Bruno. Where was he staying? Let me think. The Empress. Yes! The Empress Hotel.*

"Take me to the Empress Hotel," said Yates.

"Yes, sir," replied the driver.

Arriving at the Empress Hotel, Yates asked, "What do I owe you?"

"Ah, two dollars, sir."

Yates paid him and climbed down from the buggy with great difficulty. He entered the hotel and asked for Bruno's room number. "My man is staying here," Yates told the clerk.

After checking, the clerk replied, "Yes, sir. He stayed with us two nights, paid in advance for three, but never checked out. Let's see, I saw him Wednesday morning. Today, is Friday."

"Have you re let his room?" asked Yates.

"No sir, would you like to go up?"

"Yeah," replied Yates.

In the room he found Bruno's case and kit. The man had left and planned to return to the room, but had not. Even in his painful condition, Yates knew what that meant. Bruno was dead or in jail. "Thank you," he told the clerk. "If you don't mind, hold his things for a few days. I expect he was delayed and will be back for them."

Out on the sidewalk, Yates gave the matter some thought. If Bruno was dead, no problem, but if he was in jail, he might squeal on Yates to save himself. That, would be a problem. He decided he would go back home, to Houston and then decide his next move. He went back inside and asked the clerk when the next train to Houston was leaving.

"Sir, I'm afraid you've missed the afternoon train, but there is one leaving early in the morning."

Yates took a room and stretched out on the bed for a bit before pursuing some food. In his room, Yates realized his pocket pistol was missing, but he still had his knife. *I must get home and regroup*, he thought.

The next morning, at the train station, two city policemen approached Yates, just as he was about to board the train. "Percy Yates," said one of the officers and Yates shook his head no and turned, stepping up onto the train.

The officer grabbed his arm and pulled. The train's whistle blew. Yates jerked his arm away.

"You've got the wrong man!" hissed Yates.

The officer stepped up and grabbed Yates again and Yates hit him in the head with his cane, but the man held on. Both men tumbled to the ground, Yates dropping his cane, just as the train started moving. Yates got to his feet. His knife appeared in his hand. As the second officer tried to grab him, Yates slashed at him, cutting his arm badly. The first officer drew his revolver and shot Yates in the chest as the train pulled away.

Just before closing time, a city policeman appeared in Barlow's offices and informed him that the district attorney wanted him to know that a man by the name of Percy Yates had attacked two officers with a knife during an arrest attempt. He had been shot and was deceased. Barlow nodded and thanked the man for coming by with the information.

A few weeks later, Bruno was sentenced to three years in the Huntsville prison for assault with intent to murder; the conspiracy charge being dropped with the death of Yates. Isaac Brown recovered and took the news of Yates' death and Bruno's incarceration without clear joy.

"The world is a safer place," was all he said.

CHAPTER 29

The following week, a bank manager arrived for his appointment with Barlow. After introductions he and Barlow got down to business.

"Mr. Barlow, I manage the Big State Bank. I am here to inquire as to your interest in pursuing a debt collection for the bank. We have an employee who deals with these matters, but this is a considerable sum and I would be interested in outside help.

"Certainly," replied Barlow.

"The bank issued a Mr. Douglas Danbury funds in the amount of two-thousand dollars, some two months ago, to finance a new cattle operation. He was to acquire a bull and fifty head of cattle. A new breed from England. Herefords."

"I can't see that costing two-thousand dollars," stated Barlow.

"No, sir. The plan was that he would construct a barn, fencing, a bunkhouse, and so forth on land he owns in Galveston County on the other side of the bay. The problem is, the bank did not do its due diligence. Galveston is growing very fast and there is an exceptional amount of money being deposited and loaned out. Mr. Danbury stated he had to move quickly, and the bank did not want to miss this business opportunity. It seemed very, ah, solid. We felt that Mr. Danbury would be an important future customer when his operation grew."

"I understand your position," commented Barlow.

"Mr. Danbury missed the first payment and a bank employee visited him at this home. He told the employee that he was very sorry, but he had spent the money on drink, gambling and loose women. He stated he was almost penniless."

"I understand then, that Mr. Danbury may have committed fraud," said Barlow.

"Oh, most definitely, but again, we, ah, the bank doesn't want the embarrassment that it would face if the facts became public. Under a criminal prosecution, we fear they would. However, we thought a civil action might bear fruit. I thought to offer your firm thirty percent of any funds you are able to recover."

"Did Mr. Danbury import any cattle?" asked Barlow.

"No sir and in fact he owned little of the land he showed us. It was rented. He owns a modest home, on one hundred and sixty acres, but he has declared it as his homestead, so the bank could not get it even if we sued and won."

"All right, I'm willing to take a chance. Somehow, I doubt Mr. Danbury spent all the money in two months. I will have my assistant draw up a contract and have my investigators look into Mr. Danbury's assets. We will sue in county court and have Mr. Danbury served. I doubt he will appear for the hearing, but either way the judge should rule in the bank's favor and issue a judgement. If we can locate some assets, we'll be able to seize them."

It was Friday and before closing for the day, Phoebe informed Barlow that she was playing a part in a theater play in Galveston, and tonight was opening night. "Sadie has your best suit ready," she said.

Barlow smiled and laughed. "I wondered as to your mysterious coming and going," he said. "Ah, the mystery is solved."

Barlow and Sadie, Nathan and Elvira and of course, Tobias were in the front row for the opening night. Sadie and Elvira cried at Phoebe's amazing performance and Barlow, long a fan of the theater, was enthralled. Nathan enjoyed it immensely and Tobias beamed; the proud husband.

"I've been reading the lines of the other actors for her," he declared. "Phoebe said I did it right well."

"Look at you," said Elvira. "Getting in on the credit." Everyone laughed at Tobias' embarrassment.

CHAPTER 30

Monday morning, the Barlow team met at the café for breakfast as usual. Everyone was in good spirits. When they met after breakfast in Barlow's office, everyone setting around the table, they discussed the business at hand. It appeared to be a routine week. Phoebe was typing up two contracts for Barlow's review, a half-dozen folks had appointments for wills, Barlow had scheduled court appearances on two different probate matters and one divorce case. Also, they were pursuing the Danbury debt collection.

"Phoebe, why don't you brief everyone on the criminal cases," said Barlow.

"There are two criminal cases pending," said Phoebe. "Mr. Larson, a horse trader, has been charged with working on Sunday. He was warned once, charged the second time. He engaged Barlow to represent him and while waiting on his court date has now been charged a second time. His court date has been rescheduled per our request and will take place in two weeks. He is facing a maximum of a fifty-dollar fine for each offense. I might mention that I spoke with Mr. Larson while I was taking down his details and he insists he will continue to sell horses whenever he pleases. That said, it is possible he will face further charges prior to his court date."

"How did anyone know he was selling horses on Sunday; I mean did someone complain?" asked Nathan.

"A Mrs. Howell. Larson's neighbor. Seems she is deeply religious and was offended and shocked by his working on Sunday," explained Barlow.

Tobias smiled. "Gotta respect the man's attitude."

Phoebe frowned at Tobias.

"I just don't understand these Sunday laws. I mean, you can sell food before nine in the morning, but not after. You can sell drugs and medicine all day, but nothing else."

"The Bible says God rested on the seventh day. It's considered a day of rest and it encourages folks to go to church," replied Phoebe.

"Some businesses, considered essential can operate, for example, the stagecoaches and mail service," added Barlow.

"Restaurants are open," said Tobias and everyone nodded.

Phoebe said, "Back to business, if you please. We are representing a Mr. Robert Taylor who is facing a felony charge of burglary. In the event he is found guilty, the sentence ranges from two to twelve years in the penitentiary. His court date is next Monday. That concludes our week."

Barlow instructed Nathan and Tobias to look for Danbury's assets.

"Barlow," said Phoebe. "I should remind you. You have a meeting with the Galveston Bar Association on Friday and they will expect you to bring a draft of the bill you are working on."

Barlow looked surprised for a moment, smiled, and said, "Thank you. Oh, Sadie will be here at noon. I promised to take her to eat at Christie's. I will be back in the office by half-past one. Anyone have anything else?"

No one responded, so they all rose and began their day. Fifteen minutes before noon, Sadie emerged from Isaac's Hansom cab and entered the stairwell that ran between the bank and a land agent's office and up to Barlow's second story office. She was only a few steps up when a tremendous explosion erupted from within the bank.

Wood burst upwards in a ten-foot diameter from the floor in Barlow's outer office. Tobias and Nathan were out, but Barlow was in his office and Phoebe was at her desk. A flying chunk of wood hit Phoebe in her upper arm. Barlow dashed from his office, carrying his coat. He had just taken it from a peg on the wall in his office and was about to put it on and walk downstairs to wait for Sadie, who should arrive in ten or fifteen minutes. He ran to Phoebe's desk. She was sitting calmly, looking at her arm. Blood poured from a huge gash. Barlow reached in his coat pocket and removed a kerchief. He dropped his coat and tied the kerchief around Phoebe's arm, stemming the flow of blood.

Debris filled dust and smoke drifted into the office from the hole. "Let me help you up. We need to go downstairs," said Barlow, calmly, but firmly.

Phoebe looked at him. "My ears are ringing," she said.

"I know, come on now," said Barlow.

Barlow wrapped his arms around Phoebe and they made their way to the stairs. It was hard to tell in the haze, but they seemed to be intact. They could hear shouting from the street. As Barlow helped Phoebe onto the street, a woman took her from him. "I'll see to her."

Barlow looked at the bank. The front of it was destroyed. A horse lay dead in the street. People near the explosion had run from it, however, people hearing it were drawn to it. Women were attending to Phoebe after moving her a hundred feet away. Two men were carrying a man. Someone yelled, "I'm a doctor."

A man started into the smoke-filled bank and was met with gunfire! He staggered back out. "I'm shot," he exclaimed, falling to the wooden sidewalk. Barlow stepped over to help the man. He bent down to examine the man's wound, when a young man, wearing a soot covered suit, his face covered in blood, crawled from the wreckage inside the bank, almost reaching Barlow and the wounded man, who had just died.

"It's a hold-up," he uttered to Barlow. "They're still in there."

"How many?" asked Barlow.

"Three, but one is hurt. They blew the safe open with dynamite."

That explained the explosion, thought Barlow, rising and pulling his pistol from his shoulder holster.

"Who else is in there?" Barlow asked the young man.

"Just the owner, they have him at gunpoint."

Barlow looked around at the gathering crowd. No police officers had arrived. He rose to his feet and entered the bank. He immediately moved to his left, against the wall and squatted down, duck walking along the wall. The smoke was clearing. The counter that ran across the front lobby of the bank was largely gone.

Barlow heard voices from the back of the bank. "Help me! We can force it the rest of the way!" "We gotta git afore the law gets here!"

A loud shrieking sound followed. Then, "We done it! Help me fill the sacks!"

Barlow stood and approached the vault. Two men were standing outside the large safe, filling sacks with cash. The safe's door was mangled and bent from the dynamite blast and the pry bars they had used to pry it open. He walked past unseen; the men were focused on stealing the money. Barlow eased over to the bank owner's office. The door was partially open, but the windows were blown out. Barlow peered in and saw a man, his face and upper body soaked in blood, holding a revolver. The owner, his face covered in soot and blood, was sitting in his chair, his white shirt colored red by blood.

"Drop the gun," said Barlow, in a calm, but forceful manner.

"What the devil!" exclaimed the man, wheeling toward Barlow and pointing the gun at him.

Barlow fired one shot into the man's chest. Looking surprised, the man's mouth opened, he dropped his revolver and slumped to the floor.

"Damnit Jones!" yelled one of the men in the vault. "I told you to wait till we're leaving!"

Barlow stepped out of the owner's office and approached the two men, still busy putting the money into the feed sacks. "Idiots! Drop the sacks and raise your hands or die where you're standing," said Barlow, using his command voice.

The two men froze in place, only moving to turn their heads toward Barlow. Suddenly one dropped his sack and pulled a revolver from his waistband. At a distance of five feet, Barlow shot him in the face and swung his gun arm to cover the other robber who, on seeing his partner drop his sack had done the same. He was able to level his weapon, but before he could fire, Barlow shot him twice in the heart. The man's arm went weak and dropped as he stepped back against the safe wall and slid down it into a sitting position.

The bank's owner had his arm over Barlow's shoulder as the two made their way out of the wreckage, just as a policeman and two volunteer fireman stepped into the debris.

Barlow went in search of Phoebe and found her sitting in a buggy a block away. A doctor had sewn her arm wound closed and bandaged it. As Barlow approached, Phoebe didn't smile.

"How are you?" asked Barlow.

"Barlow. Sadie must have arrived just as the explosion occurred. She is injured. I had her taken to Doctor Evans office."

Barlow stood perfectly still, his mind racing. It had only been ten minutes since the explosion erupted, and he had not imagined that Sadie would have yet arrived to go to dinner with him. "Thank you," he said.

Barlow found a man who agreed to take him to Dr. Evans' office. There he found the doctor busy treating Sadie. Barlow stood, grim-faced, watching. Finally, the doctor stepped back and noticed Barlow.

"Sam, she hasn't spoken, but cried out in pain. There is a large knot on her head. Her shoulder was out of joint and her leg is broken. She has some cuts. I've set her leg, forced her shoulder into place and treated her wounds. I don't know about her head. We'll have to give it time. I decided not to give her laudanum, but she is in pain, so I've given her some morphine. She'll sleep for hours. It's best if you leave her here for a while, so I can watch her."

CHAPTER 31

The Barlow law office was closed for two days while repairs were completed to the structure of the building and the hole in the office floor was repaired. Sadie continued to improve and was moved home. Phoebe hired a nurse to care for her on a full-time basis until she recovered.

On the third day, Barlow was at the courthouse when the district attorney saw him. "Barlow, how's Mrs. Barlow faring?" he asked.

"She's coming along, thank you," replied Barlow.

"Excellent. Wonderful news. You might be interested in this. One of the bank robbers, the one who was holding the bank owner in his office, lived for an hour," said the district attorney. "One of the officers that responded asked him what happened. Seems they boiled some dynamite and skimmed the powder-oil off it."

Barlow frowned.

"Nitro-glycerin," said the district attorney. The vault door had groves in it and after they pried the door a bit, they were going to burn through them with the powder-oil, but somehow, they messed it up and was in a hurry, so they stuck some dynamite in the crack and well, you know the rest. Any no how, you saved me a passel of work by dealing with the three brigands. See you in court, Barlow."

Barlow had tried to convince Phoebe to stay home for a few days, to recover, but she refused. Tobias and Nathan were in Houston tracking down Danbury's assets - the man who had defaulted on his loans from the bank. Barlow and Phoebe handled the week's work while working on a defense for Robert Taylor, charged with felony burglary.

Nathan and Tobias had successfully completed their mission by the end of the week, but Barlow had a meeting with the Galveston Bar Association and was finishing up his preparations for Robert Taylor's trial on Monday, so they didn't see him. He told Phoebe he would not be in the office on Saturday, but would spend the day with Sadie, who was recovering, but still in pain.

"She wants me to read to her," said Barlow.

"As well you should, Barlow," replied Phoebe.

Monday morning, Barlow and Phoebe were in court to defend Robert Taylor on burglary charges. Twenty-four names were drawn for prospective jurors and Barlow looked the names over as they were handed to him and felt no need to challenge any of them. The defense had the right to strike up to ten names and the state five. The district attorney challenged two that he knew and thought might lean toward the defense, no matter what the facts. The judge seated a jury of twelve men.

The indictment of Robert Taylor for burglary was read to the jury. Mr. Taylor entered a plea of not guilty to the judge. The district attorney presented his case.

"Gentlemen of the jury, the defendant is charged with burglary. A most serious endeavor. He was caught red-handed standing in the kitchen of Mr. and Mrs. Clemson in the early morning hours with their silver tea-pot in his hands. Now, in his statement to the sheriff, Mr. Taylor claimed he entered the Clemson house by mistake and was only admiring the tea-pot," stated the district attorney, who chuckled at the absurdity of the statement.

Barlow watched serenely, but the judge spoke up. "Mr. District Attorney."

"My apologies your honor."

The district attorney called Mr. Clemson as a witness. After Mr. Clemson was administered the oath, the district attorney approached.

"Good morning, Mr. Clemson. Can you tell the court what transpired, ah, what happened in your very own kitchen during the early morning hours of May 2nd?

"I sure as hell can," exclaimed Clemson.

"Language," said the judge.

"Sorry, your honor. Well, the rooster crowed. Now that don't mean nothing cause that rooster crows whenever he feels like it, but any no how, I looked at my pocket watch. I keep it beside the bed at night, you see. It were ten minutes past six, so I got on up although the sun don't rise this time a year till half past. I milk the cow every morning at day-break. I didn't light the lantern because Martha, my wife, was still sleeping. Well, sir, I heard a noise. I grabbed my scattergun. I keep it beside the bed. I eased the door open and stepped into the kitchen. There stood a man, holding my wife's silver tea-pot. I told him not to move, 'cept to put the tea-pot down. I called for my boy, he's twelve, and sent him to fetch my neighbor. We stood there me and the fellow until my neighbor came. My neighbor trussed the fellow up and helped me put him in the wagon. I took him to the sheriff's station in Clear Creek."

"Is the man you found in your kitchen in this courtroom?" asked the district attorney.

"Yes sir. It's the fellow sitting right there," he said, pointing at Robert Taylor.

"Thank you Mr. Clemson," said the district attorney. "I have concluded my questioning of the witness, your honor."

"Mr. Barlow. Did you have questions?" asked the judge.

"I do your honor," said Barlow, standing.

"Do you bar your doors at night, Mr. Clemson?" asked Barlow.

"I do," replied Clemson.

"Did you bar them before retiring on the night in question?"

"I did," answered Clemson.

"I see, however, you discovered Mr. Taylor in your kitchen. How was he able to enter your home without waking you?"

Clemson scratched his beard. "Well sir, it were hot, so I opened the kitchen window while Martha was cooking my supper. I reckon I forgot to close it."

"Now, Mr. Clemson, you stated you looked at your watch and the time was ten past six, is that correct?"

"That's what I said," responded Clemson, a bit of anger in his voice.

"When you heard the noise, had you dressed?"

Clemson thought for a moment. "I had my trousers and boots on."

"You rose at ten past the hour and pulled on your trousers and boots and then heard the noise. Is that correct?" asked Barlow.

"What the devil does it matter?" exclaimed Clemson. "I caught the man in my kitchen with the tea-pot in his hand!"

Barlow smiled. "Please answer the question, sir."

"Yes, yes, yes. I got up, pulled on my trousers and boots and heard the noise in the kitchen."

"No more questions, your honor."

The district attorney stood. "Your honor, need I call Mrs. Clemson to verify it was in fact Mr. Taylor in their kitchen?"

The judge looked at Barlow. "Your honor, we concede the fact that Mr. Taylor was the man in the Clemson kitchen."

"In that case, the prosecution rests," stated the district attorney, smiling.

"I have a question for Mr. Clemson," stated the judge. "Mr. Clemson, when you discovered Mr. Taylor in your kitchen holding your wife's tea-pot, why didn't you shoot him on the spot? 'Texas Justice', some would call it."

"I would have, your honor, without a thought, but I was afraid I'd damage the tea-pot, and I'd have the devil to pay for that when my wife saw it."

Laughter broke out in the courtroom and the judge tapped his gavel, "All right, all right now," he said, trying not to smile himself.

Barlow stood and with a voice that was filled with confidence, said, "Mr. Taylor did not commit the crime of burglary for which he has been charged." He paused. Silence filled the courtroom. "The honorable district attorney pointed out in his opening that Mr. Taylor explained he entered the Clemson's home by mistake and was admiring their tea-pot when discovered by Mr. Clemson. I will show this statement to be fact in my presentation."

"The defense calls the defendant, Robert Taylor," said Barlow, in a clear, loud voice.

Taylor was sworn in and sat in the witness chair. Barlow approached. "Mr. Taylor, can you tell the court what you did on the evening of May 1st?"

"Ah, my wife went to spend the night with her sister in Houston, so I thought I'd take the opportunity and do some socializing myself. I went to the saloon in Clear Creek."

"What time did you leave the saloon?" asked Barlow.

"I ain't sure, but likely about midnight. Henry, my friend Henry Hughes, he said he had some moonshine, so we left and went to his place.

117

We sat on his porch and drank shine for a bit. We fell asleep. I woke up, and it were still dark, but I figured I better get on home. I got chores has to be done early. I got home, but the door were barred. I figured my wife must have decided not to spend the night at her sisters' and was mad. She would have guessed I was off drinking. I walked around back, but I seen the kitchen window was wide open, so I climbed in. When I got in I seen a silver tea-pot. I wondered how in the world we got a silver tea-pot. Her sister weren't likely to give us one."

A few chuckles could be heard in the courtroom. The judge glared.

"Please continue Mr. Taylor," said Barlow.

"Well sir, I was studying the tea-pot when a fellow with a scattergun told me to put it down and stay put. We just stood there for a bit. He sent his boy to fetch his neighbor. When it got light, I could see I was in the wrong house."

The district attorney's assistant was whispering in his ear. The district attorney frowned. The district attorney leafed through the criminal code book laying on the desk beside him.

"Mr. District Attorney," said the judge.

"No questions," replied the district attorney, his face pale.

"Your honor, the defense rests and we have a motion," said Barlow.

"Let's hear it," said the judge.

"Your honor, we request a dismissal of all charges. The state has failed to show that the defendant committed the crime of burglary."

"Don't you think that's for the jury to decide?" asked the judge.

"Your honor, if I might, to clarify my motion, read the statute on burglary?"

"I object," said the district attorney, but not with much force.

"I suppose so Mr. Barlow," replied the judge, "but just the parts that apply to your motion."

"*... it is not necessary that there should be any actual breaking to constitute the offense of burglary, except when the entry is made in the daytime.*"

"Now, your honor, I read this to mean that during the day-time, some force must be used to gain entry for a person to be charged with burglary. Mr. Taylor did not use force, he did not raise the window. He simply climbed in the open window."

"It was dark!" exclaimed the district attorney.

"I agree," said Barlow. "If you will allow, Mr. District Attorney, that will be addressed in short order. Now, if I may continue, '*By the term "breaking," as used in article 705, is meant "Breaking" that the entry must be made with actual force. The slightest force, however, is sufficient to constitute breaking; it may be by lifting the latch of the door that is shut, or by raising a window, the entry at a chimney, or other unusual place...*" Barlow paused.

"I contend that Mr. Taylor entered the house during the daytime and that he did not use force of any kind. He did not raise a window. He simply climbed in an open window. Now, as for the fact it was dark, I point the court and the jury to ART. 710, which states: '*By the term " day-time " is meant any time of the twenty-four hours <u>from thirty minutes before sunrise</u> until thirty minutes after sunset.*' End of code. Now, Mr. Clemson has testified that he checked his watch at ten minutes past six, pulled on his trousers and boots and heard a sound in the kitchen. I contend that sunrise on May2nd was, give or take a minute or two, half-past six. Mr. Taylor climbed in the window at say, fifteen minutes past six. Thus, he entered the house during what is defined legally, as daytime."

"Well now, Mr. Barlow, you've cut your point mighty fine, but you made a point. However, we're going to let the jury decide the facts and interpret the law," announced the judge.

Barlow walked to within a few feet of the jury and said, "Gentlemen, there are two issues here. The first is simple common sense. Robert Taylor had been drinking most of the night. He mistook Mr. Clemson's house for his own in the dark. He climbed in an open window. He was amazed to find a silver tea-pot in the kitchen. He had no sack with him in which to put stolen items because he is not a thief. Second, the law states that if you are to be charged with burglary and it is committed during the day-time, you must have completed some act of force in entering the premises. Mr. Taylor did not use force of any kind to enter the house. It was dark, you say. Yes, it was dark. That is why he mistook this home for his own. But the law defines day-time as beginning thirty-minutes before sunrise. Mr. Taylor clearly entered the Clemson home after six in the morning. Less than thirty-minutes before sunrise. You must find him not guilty under the law. Thank you."

Having the final say, the district attorney rose and said, "Gentlemen. Common sense tells us if a man enters a home when it is dark and takes hold of a valuable silver tea-pot belonging to someone else, he is up to no good. All this talk about time. It was dark. Mr. Taylor entered the house at night. Do your duty and find Mr. Taylor guilty as charged."

The judge gave his instructions to the jury, and they retired to consider.

While they waited, Barlow turned to Phoebe and said, "Phoebe, you did excellent work researching the law. It's the first time I've had a case like this. Normally, if someone is caught inside another's home, he's shot on the spot."

"Thanks, Barlow," she replied, with a rare smile.

Twenty minutes later the jury returned with a not guilty verdict.

CHAPTER 32

Phoebe finally let Tobias and Nathan in to see Barlow mid-afternoon. The office had been busy and Phoebe wasn't one to turn away potential clients.

"Tobias, Nathan," said Barlow, greeting the two men.

After the two were seated, Tobias said, "We've a report on Mr. Danbury, the fellow that told the bank he had drank, gambled and spent all the money he borrowed."

"Excellent," replied Barlow.

Tobias continued, "We checked the land records in Galveston and Harris counties, but didn't find any property belonging to Mr. Danbury, other than his homestead. However, we checked the cattle and horse brand records, being as how he said he was going to buy some cattle."

Tobias and Nathan both smiled.

"Of course, we didn't expect to find anything, but low and behold there was a new brand registered. The double D is registered to a Mr. Douglas Danbury. After we discovered that, we waited outside his house. When he left, we followed him northwest into Fort Bend County. We used a looking glass and spotted a bull and three or four dozen cows. Funny looking critters. Short-horns. They sported the DD brand. The land belongs to a Mr. Henderson, whom we contacted and we were informed the land had been rented to Mr. Danbury."

"Do tell," said Barlow, smiling. "They must be that new breed, Herefords."

Nathan took up the narrative. "When he left the ranch, he rode to Houston. Stopped in a bank there."

"Good work. He's likely deposited his borrowed money in the new bank. At least what he hasn't spent yet. We have a court date tomorrow.

Even if he shows up, which I doubt, we'll get a judgement. That done, you two can take it to the sheriff and visit the bank and the ranch where the cattle are being held and have the sheriff seize everything."

Phoebe appeared in the doorway. "Barlow, a boy is here with a note. The judge wants to know if he can hear the Larson case tomorrow. He's going fishing next week."

"Let's see, Larson, the fellow accused of selling horses on Sunday. Tell the judge yes and send Tobias or Nathan to see Larson and tell him."

The following morning, in the Justice of the Peace court, an assistant district attorney was present to prosecute Larson for conducting business on Sunday. He was charged with two counts and facing a possible fine of fifty dollars for each count.

"If your honor please," said Barlow. "Mr. Larson would like his case tried without a jury. Just before your honor, a bench trial."

"Wonderful, that will speed things along considerably," replied the judge.

After a brief opening statement, the assistant district attorney called the complaining witness, Mrs. Howell, to testify.

Mrs. Howell stated, "I witnessed Mr. Larson selling horses on two different Sundays. I saw Larson showing the horses, the men riding them, I saw them shake hands. It was obvious," said Mrs. Howell. "An affront to the good Lord's Day."

The next prosecution witness was a deputy sheriff. After he was sworn in the prosecutor asked him, "Deputy, did you ride out to the Larson place and investigate Mrs. Howell's accusation, that Larson was working on Sunday, selling horses."

"I did."

"And what did you discover?"

"I asked Larson about it and he confirmed he had been working on Sunday, but when I asked him what work he did on Sunday, he told me it were none of my business."

When the prosecutor had finished presenting his case, Barlow made a motion that the charges be dismissed.

"Mr. Barlow. On what grounds are you asking the charges be dismissed?" asked the judge, clearly puzzled.

"Your Honor, Mr. Larson operates a livery. The law makes an exception for certain necessary businesses, including liveries, so he was not breaking the Sunday law by operating on Sunday."

The prosecutor leapt to his feet. "Your honor! I object. Mr. Larson's place of business is located out in the county and it is not a livery. It's only a horse-trading business. He doesn't rent out horses."

"Mr. Barlow, what say we talk to Mr. Larson?"

"Fine, your honor," said Barlow, waving at Larson to come up and take the oath.

"Mr. Larson, you understand the penalty for lying under oath," said the judge.

"I do."

"How many horses have you under your care at the livery at this moment?"

"One, that don't belong to me. Six that do."

"I see. So do you rent out these horses?" asked the judge.

"Why your honor, I am always willing to rent out horses. Would you be needing to rent one?" asked Larson.

The judge smiled. "How many horses have you rented out in the last month?"

"Two, your honor."

The judge sat back, thinking. Barlow stood. "May I speak your honor?"

"What is it, Barlow?"

"I don't think the law states how much business a livery has to conduct in order to qualify as a livery."

After a minute of reflection, the judge, said, "Case dismissed," slamming his gavel down.

Tobias and Nathan had attended the hearing and Tobias leaned over and said, "I wondered why Barlow had us rent horses from Larson last week."

Mrs. Howell stormed out of the courtroom, her face flaming red.

CHAPTER 33

The Danbury Herefords were seized by the sheriff as was nine hundred dollars from Danbury's bank account in Houston. The cattle and bull were a novelty and at auction brought a premium of eight hundred dollars. The Barlow firm earned five hundred and ten dollars from the debt collection, which pleased Phoebe immensely.

Tobias and Phoebe looked into buying a buggy and were shocked at the cost, nearly thirty dollars for a new one. Phoebe decided a used one would work just fine. Tobias knew they could afford a new one; they were both well paid. Barlow paid Phoebe the incredible amount of one hundred and five dollars a month. He was paid eighty dollars a month himself, but Phoebe was conservative and they put money in savings every month. Sadie had told Phoebe that she purchased a walnut wardrobe for Barlow and it cost nearly twenty dollars. Phoebe was shocked that someone would pay so much for a wardrobe, even if it was walnut.

Sadie healed and business flourished as the year turned into summer. Everyone was busy, prospering and enjoying life on the island. But events beyond their control were unfolding.

Two men were at the Wild Horse Saloon, drinking beer and arguing. Harlan, a hard looking man who had recently been released from Huntsville Penitentiary after serving two years for assault, was sitting at a table with his younger brother, Bert, a thin man, whose hollow cheeks gave the impression of a skeleton. Bert was a heroin addict who made his living by stealing. His favorite hunting grounds, was along the pier at night. It was dangerous because the wares waiting to be loaded or transported inland were guarded, but Bert was careful and never tried for too much.

"Harlan, if the man was so damn good why was he in prison with you?" demanded Bert.

"His woman gave him up," said Harlan. "Which reminds me. We don't tell no one our plans. I mean no one, Bert and especially no women. They can't be trusted."

"What are you going on about? We ain't got no plan. We're just talking and I'm saying I don't like what you're saying," said Bert.

"Is that a fact? How much money you got?"

"Well, I got about four dollars," replied Bert.

"Four dollars. A time we drink a little and get a bite, it'll be mite near gone," said Harlan.

"I'm going down to the docks tonight. It's cloudy and them lights don't cover everywhere," said Bert.

"How much you usually get; you go down to the docks?"

"Well, it depends on what I find, you know. The man what buys my stuff, he don't give me much, but I been getting five or six dollars for what I can carry off."

"That's what I thought. I'm telling you, this guy said on his last job, he got two hundred dollars, cash," declared Harlan.

"Two hundred dollars!" exclaimed Bert.

"That's right. Now all we need is a rich man. We'll kidnap his wife. Who do you know, that's rich?"

"Harlan, how am I going to know any rich people?"

"You don't have to know them, just know who they are and where we can find 'em," said Harlan.

"You know, I was thinking. A while back, me and Willie was doing the bump and grab and some misdirection, you know, tapping a few pockets, when the theatre let out. All them fancy dressed people and all. Well, there was this little crowd formed around the door and this real beautiful woman come out and I asked somebody there who she was. They said an actress in the play. I told well, I never knew of her and they say, oh, she lives in Galveston and works for the lawyer Mr. Barlow when she ain't acting. See, last time I was in jail, I heard of this Barlow. Lots of fellows would like to hire him, but he's expensive and choosy about who he defends and all."

"Hellfire Burt! An actress. That's great! Now, see. All we gotta do is find his office and follow this female helper of his; this actress. We'll grab her and send this lawyer a note, saying we want two hundred dollars are we're gonna kill her," explained Harlan.

"What if he don't pay?" asked Bert.

"Don't worry about that. My friend said they always pay when you snatch a woman," answered Harlan.

CHAPTER 34

Harlan and Bert waited across the street from Barlow's law office. They stood, smoking, talking, trying to act like they belonged.

The sun set and the gas lamps were lit before Phoebe and Tobias appeared out of the stairwell leading to Barlow's offices. Phoebe had been working late, typing a document and Tobias waited with her. Barlow was still in his office, researching court decisions and Nathan was working undercover in a warehouse. The owner, a client of Barlow's, was losing goods and hired Barlow to discover which of his employees was stealing from him.

As Phoebe and Tobias stepped into the night, Tobias's hat blew off and his shoulder length hair blew in the wind. He caught his hat and jammed it back on, as Phoebe laughed.

Harlan and Bert were startled when they saw Tobias's long hair. "I don't reckon we need fear that girly fellow," said Harlan. "I'll take care of him; you grab the girl. Let's go."

Harlan and Bert followed the couple who had walked home, as the night was mild and the ocean brought a pleasant breeze through the city. As Tobias and Phoebe started up the steps of their home, Bert grabbed Phoebe from behind, one hand over her mouth as he roughly jerked her backwards and dragged her away, into the darkness. Hearing her muffled cries, Tobias turned just as Harlan, brandishing a knife, stepped toward him.

Tobias, standing on the porch, Harlan two steps below him, kicked Harlan in the chest, sending him toppling backward, landing on his back. Meanwhile, Phoebe sank her teeth into Bert's hand, causing him to scream and release his hold on her. She turned and slammed her fist into his nose. Bert screamed again and grabbed his nose with both hands. Phoebe kicked him, hard, in his manhood and he fell to the ground, curled in a ball and groaned and whimpered.

Harlan scrambled to his feet just as Tobias reached him, his own knife in his hand. The two men circled each other. Harlan slashed right and left with his knife, but missed as Tobias stepped and twisted away. Harlan lunged, but Tobias, who had been shanghaied and was forced to serve on a ship to Asia, had become an expert at knife fighting and un-armed combat. Tobias slashed Harlan's arm and Harlan's knife fell to the ground.

Tobias dropped his own knife, and stepped toward Harlan. Grabbing Harlan's wounded arm with his right hand, Tobias raised the arm, turned his back on Harland and brought Harlan's arm down, hard on his own right shoulder, breaking Harlan's arm. As Harlan screamed in pain, Tobias let go of him, turned and hit the man in the face. Once, twice and Harlan went down.

A neighbor, hearing the commotion appeared with a revolver in his hand. "What's happened?" asked the neighbor.

"These men attacked us," said Phoebe.

"I've some rope, I'll fetch it," said the neighbor.

In a few minutes Harland and Bert, both alternately groaning and cursing, were securely tied with rope and the neighbor had left to fetch the city marshal.

An hour later, two deputy marshals had loaded the men in a police wagon and taken them away.

Chapter 35

Hearing of the assault on Phoebe and Tobias, Barlow had been appalled, but they had assured him they were fine. Nathan caught the man stealing from his employer and the law firm became busier than ever.

Two weeks later, Barlow and Sadie hosted supper for Phoebe, Tobias, Nathan and Elvira. The group dined on fresh fish and vegetables with pie for dessert. After supper, the ladies adjourned to the sewing room to look at a quilt that Sadie was making. The men trouped up to Barlow's study where they stood on a balcony, smoking cigars and drinking coffee. They could see the Gulf of Mexico from their perch.

"It's been an eventful year," said Barlow.

Tobias and Nathan laughed. "I think you might have understated it a bit, boss," he said.

Downstairs, as the women praised Sadie's quilt, she told them she had some news. "I haven't told Sam yet," she said. "I'm pregnant."

Phoebe and Elvira gasped.

Upstairs, Tobias, Nathan and Barlow stood silently, smoking and sipping their coffee. Each with his own thoughts as they looked out over the ocean.

The End

Made in United States
Troutdale, OR
07/05/2024

21026364R00087